9/13

To Be
PERFECTLY
Honest

Also by Sonya Sones

What My Mother Doesn't Know
One of Those Hideous Books Where the Mother Dies
What My Girlfriend Doesn't Know
Stop Pretending

To Be PERFECTLY Honest

A Novel Based on an *Untrue* Story

SONYA SONES

SIMON & SCHUSTER BFYR

New York   London   Toronto   Sydney   New Delhi

SIMON & SCHUSTER BFYR

An imprint of Simon & Schuster Children's Publishing Division
1230 Avenue of the Americas, New York, New York 10020
This book is a work of fiction. Any references to historical events,
real people, or real places are used fictitiously. Other names, characters,
places, and events are products of the author's imagination,
and any resemblance to actual events or places or persons,
living or dead, is entirely coincidental.

For information about special discounts for bulk purchases, please
contact Simon & Schuster Special Sales at 1-866-506-1949 or
business@simonandschuster.com.
The Simon & Schuster Speakers Bureau can bring authors
to your live event. For more information or to book an event, contact the
Simon & Schuster Speakers Bureau at 1-866-248-3049 or
visit our website at www.simonspeakers.com.
Book design by Hilary Zarycky
The text for this book is set in New Caledonia.
Manufactured in the United States of America
2 4 6 8 10 9 7 5 3 1
Library of Congress Cataloging-in-Publication Data
Sones, Sonya.
To be perfectly honest : a novel based on an untrue story / Sonya
Sones.—First edition.
pages cm
Summary: Fifteen-year-old Colette is a compulsive liar spending a
miserable summer in San Luis Obispo, California, babysitting her seven-
year-old brother while her famous mother shoots a movie, but things look
up when Connor enters the scene.
ISBN 978-0-689-87604-2 (hardcover)
ISBN 978-1-4424-9477-0 (eBook)
[1. Honesty—Fiction. 2. Brothers and sisters—Fiction.
3. Dating (Social customs)—Fiction. 4. Fame—Fiction.
5. Single-parent families—Fiction. 6. San Luis Obispo (Calif.) —
Fiction.] I. Title.
PZ7.S6978To 2013
[Fic]—dc23
2012048563

FIRST
EDITION

To Ruth Bornstein, Peg Leavitt,
Betsy Rosenthal, Ann Wagner,
and April Halprin Wayland—
for always telling me the truth.

Acknowledgments

Many, many people deserve my undying gratitude for holding my hand, cheering me on, sharing their brilliance, and providing safe haven while I wandered through the tunnel without a flashlight—my agent, Steven Malk; my husband, Bennett Tramer; my children, Ava and Jeremy; my ladies of the pink kitchen; and, of course, my third acters. Thanks also to David Gale and Justin Chanda for their patience; to Myra Cohn Livingston for teaching me everything I know; to my readers for writing me such lovely letters; and to my friends, Richard Peck, Gayle Forman, Ron Koertge, and Amy Ness for being there when I needed them. And a huge hug to all the welcoming folks at my secret office—I couldn't have done it without the shade, the view, the chair, and the plug.

"Beauty is truth, truth beauty."
—John Keats

"Truth is beautiful, without doubt; but so are lies."
—Ralph Waldo Emerson

To Be
PERFECTLY
Honest

They Tell Me There Was an Accident

Though I can't
remember it happening.
Here's what I do remember:

I remember climbing into a limo
with my little brother Will to visit our mom
on the set of her latest film.

It smelled
like someone had been
smoking pot in there.

Or maybe drinking champagne.
Or throwing up.
Or all three.

Sort of like
our living room
after one of Mom's all-night parties.

I remember
rolling down the window
for some breathable air

while Will bounced around,
like he always does
when we're in a limo,

telling me
one goofy knock-knock joke
after another.

I remember turning onto Sunset Boulevard,
and seeing a massive billboard
of a guy wearing nothing but jeans—

his fly unzipped
just low enough
to make me look twice.

Will saw it too.
He grinned at me and lisped through the gap
where his baby teeth used to be, "Thex thells!"

Sex sells?
How does a seven-year-old even *know* that?
I was just about to ask him—

but I never got the chance.

Because That's When
the Cop Car Appeared

It came out of nowhere
and latched onto our tail
like a rabid dog.

I glanced into the rearview mirror—
our driver's eyes looked like they were
getting ready to pop right out of their sockets.

He started swearing
in a language I've never heard before,
then flung a package out the window.

I began shouting at him,
telling him he better pull over
and let us out *right now*!

But the guy just
whipped out a gun,
waved it wildly in our direction,

then turned back around
and slammed his foot down hard
on the gas.

Suddenly

We were in
one of those high-speed chases
like you see on TV—

zooming down one-way streets the wrong way,
careening around corners,
running red lights.

Then there were *two* police cars chasing us.
Then there were three.
Then four.

Will was squeezing my hand so hard it hurt.
But he was laughing and whooping and hollering
like we were riding a roller coaster.

I was squeezing *his* hand too,
my heart kickboxing
against my ribs.

Then I heard a rumbling above us.
I stuck my head out the window and saw
a helicopter with a cameraman hanging out of it.

I pulled my iPhone out of my purse
and a second later my brother and I were watching
our own personal drama unfold on CNN.

Will sucked in a breath.
"Colette . . . ," he said, in this real awestruck voice.
"We're on . . . *TV!*"

It Was So Surreal It Wasn't Even Funny

We looked up at the sky
and watched the guy
filming us,

then we looked down at my phone
and saw the footage
he was shooting.

For a few minutes,
we got so into
watching the chase,

that we almost forgot
we were the ones
being chased.

But then the camera pulled back
and Will and I could see
that there were six cop cars tailing us now,

like we were all
in some crazy motorcade
rushing to get to a funeral on time.

I hoped it wouldn't be *ours* . . .

Then the Camera Pulled Back
Even Further

And we saw
that in about half a mile
the road would lead us onto a bridge . . .

A bridge that would carry us over a river . . .
A river so dark and wide and churning
that it looked more like an ocean . . .

Then our driver started swearing again.
Will and I glanced up
from my phone—

and that was when we saw
that the bridge we were bearing down on
was under construction.

And that halfway across the river,
it simply

stopped.

The Very Last Thing I Remember

Is grabbing Will
and wrapping my arms around him

just as the limo
slammed through a wooden barrier.

Then that sick feeling you get
from a sudden drop,

and Will screaming,
"To infinity and beyond!"

After that,
nothing—

no memory
of hitting the river,

no memory of the icy black water
filling my lungs.

But I know
it must have.

Because . . .
well . . . because . . .

I'm dead.

So What's It Like to Be Dead?

Well, the best part is
that up here you don't have to worry
about anything.

In fact,
you *can't* worry about anything.
Even when you try.

I can't even worry
about what happened
to Will.

So, mostly, I just hang out
on this comfy cloud couch
in the sky

(they get pretty cute
with that cloud motif
up here),

eating perfectly buttered,
perfectly salted popcorn
from a bowl that never gets empty,

while watching Earthtube—
which is sort of like a live streaming video
of the whole world.

If, for instance, I want to see
what my BFFs, Crystal, Bette, and Madison,
are up to,

or if I want to find out
if Ruby and Wyatt are still hooking up,
all I have to do is whisper their names,

then click this golden remote,
and their lives come up like a movie
on my screen—

as though the entire planet
is just one big huge reality show,
starring whoever I *want* it to star.

It's *heaven.*

Or at Least It's How I *Imagine* Heaven to Be

Though
I have no way of knowing
what it's *really* like.

Because
I, myself,
am *not* dead.

None of that stuff
I told you about just now
actually happened.

Aw, come on.
Did you honestly think
I was dead

and, like,
beaming this story down to you
from heaven?

Then
you're even easier to fool
than I thought.

Though I'm Sorry I Misled You

Really.
I *am.*

But once I get going,
once I start reinventing reality

and spinning it off
in a whole new direction,

it's damn near impossible
for me to stop.

Though the truth is,
I mean the real honest-to-God truth

about why I can't seem to keep myself
from . . . exaggerating,

is that my actual life
sucks.

Big time.

Why Does My Life Suck?

Why does it *suck*?
Well . . . because . . .
Well . . . I'm a vampire.

And once a month,
in the middle of the night,
when the full moon rises over the lonely moor,

I wake
with a raging thirst
clawing at my throat—

a thirst
that can only be quenched
by one thing.

So I rise up
from my coffin
and lurch out into the night . . .

to
buy
some Dr Pepper.

(Sorry. I couldn't resist.)

But Seriously

The real reason my life sucks
is that my father's a dogcatcher
and my mother's a meter maid.

Actually, that's not true.
My father's a clown
and my mother's a trapeze artist.

Actually, that's not true either.
I don't have a clue who my father is
and my mother's a famous movie star.

Actually, that *is* true.
Though I wouldn't blame you
if you didn't believe me.

Because, as you might have noticed,
I like to strrrrrrrrrretch the truth a bit.
I like to enhance . . . embroider . . . embellish . . .

I guess
what I'm trying to say
is this:

I
am a big fat
liar.

Lying's What I Do

I'm sort of known
for it.

The kids at school
even have a joke about me:

How can you tell
if Colette is lying?

Her mouth
is open.

In Fact

I'm what
your English teacher
calls an "unreliable narrator."

And I'm what
Crystal, Bette, and Madison
call an unreliable friend.

They call me
much worse than that,
actually.

Though only when one of my lies backfires
and nearly gets us all expelled or arrested
or something.

But that hardly ever happens.
Because I'm just so darn good at it.
Or, as my mother's fond of saying:

"Colette, darling,
Pinocchio's skills pale
in comparison to yours."

And I've got to admit she's right—
just about the only true thing
you'll ever hear me say is this:

You can't believe a word I say.

The Liar's Paradox

If a person says
"You can't believe a word I say,"
is her statement true or false?

If her statement is true,
then everything *in* her statement
has to be true. Right?

But, because her statement
tells us we can't believe
a word she says,

then everything in her statement
has to be false.
Right?

So—
which is it:
true or false?

Sort of
makes your head hurt,
doesn't it?

These are the kinds of things I think about.
When I'm not busy thinking about
how pitiful my life is.

Why Is My Life So Pitiful?

Because,
like I told you a few pages ago—
my mother is a famous movie star.

Yeah, yeah.
I know what you're thinking:
That's just more of Colette's BS.

But guess what?
When I told you that you couldn't believe
a word I said—I was lying.

You *can* believe
some of what I say.
So go ahead and Google it if you want.

You'll find out
who my mother is
in two seconds flat.

Oh, What the Heck

You don't have to bother
Googling it.

I'll just tell you myself
and get it over with:

My mother
is Marissa Shawn.

Yes.
That Marissa Shawn.

The one who starred
in all those blockbusters

with George Clooney and Johnny Depp
and Brad Pitt,

the one who's got three Golden Globes
and two Oscars displayed on the mantel,

the one who's more talented,
more beautiful,

more
just plain awesome

than I
will *ever* be.

That's Why I Made All That Stuff Up

About the car chase and being dead.
That's why I *always* make stuff up—
to try to make myself seem
more fascinating than I actually am.

At least that's what my shrink says.
Because the problem with being
Marissa Shawn's daughter
is that no one is interested in *me*.

And I mean *no* one.
Once people find out
who my mother is,
they all want to be my best friend.

But after that,
I'm never really sure
if it's *me* they like
or just the fact that *she's* my mother.

Oh, wait.
I *am* sure—
it's just the fact
that she's my mother.

It's All About Her—It Always Is

"Oooo . . .
What's Marissa Shawn really like?"

"Was that your *mom's* butt in that last movie,
or did she use a body double?"

"Did she really have three ribs removed
to make her waist look smaller?"

"Is it true she's secretly hooking up
with Justin Bieber?"

Geez . . . Can you hear
my eyes rolling up into their sockets?

Only idiots believe everything
they read in the *National Enquirer*.

Unfortunately,
most people are idiots.

But For the Record:

That *was* a body double.
(Though you didn't hear that from *me*.)

And she only had
one rib removed.

And give me
a break—

she's hooking up with John Mayer.
Not Justin Bieber.

Though even Mayer's
way too young for her.

Not that that's ever
stopped her before.

Oh, Whoops

I forgot to answer that first question:
"Oooo . . . What's Marissa Shawn really like?"

Marissa Shawn is the kind of person
who could never be satisfied

with being loved by one measly man
and a couple of kids.

She has to be loved
by the masses.

Marissa Shawn is the kind of person
who's so narcissistic

that she can't focus
for more than a couple of minutes at a time

on anyone
but herself.

Marissa Shawn is the kind of person
who strolls into my bedroom

the day after my summer vacation begins
and says things like,

"Guess what? DreamWorks just asked me
to star in a comedy called *Love Canoe*.

So throw a few things into a suitcase, darling.
You and Will are coming on location with me!"

Even though she knows for a fact
that this will ruin my life.

Why Will This Ruin My Life?

Well, first of all,
Love Canoe is shooting in San Luis Obispo.

Which is halfway up
the coast of California,

somewhere between Boringtown
and Nowheresville.

I just checked Wikipedia,
and believe me—

there is less than nothing
to do there.

I mean, the most exciting event of the week
is the farmers' market.

Need I say more?

Actually, I Think I *Do* Need
to Say More:

San Luis Obispo
is 190 miles from Los Angeles,
230 miles from San Francisco,
and a zillion miles from Paris,

which is where
my mother owns a house
that's bigger
than the Louvre—

the house where I
was supposed to be
hanging out all summer
with Crystal, Bette, and Madison.

That is,
when we weren't busy sailing
from Nice to Cannes to Saint-Tropez
on our yacht.

I Told My Mother

There was no way in hell
I'd go on location with her.
I told her she couldn't do this
to me and my friends.

I told her
I'd rather die
than spend the summer
in San Luis Obispo.

But she told me
to accept my fate,
pack a bag,
and get in the goddamn car.

Which Is Where I Am Right Now

Being kidnapped
by my own mother.

DreamWorks offered her a limo,
but naturally she turned them down.

She told them
she'd rather drive us up herself—

in her
look-at-me-I'm-saving-the-planet Prius.

She wanted me to ride shotgun.
But I flat out refused.

So I'm sitting next to Will in the backseat,
giving our mother the silent treatment.

She's acting all
lighthearted and chatty,

amusing herself
by pretending to be our tour guide—

pointing out every barn we pass,
every bale of hay and blade of grass.

I'm amusing myself by tossing imaginary
poison darts at the back of her head.

Will thinks this
is a riot.

But Will Thinks *Everything* I Do Is a Riot

He thinks
I'm the greatest thing
since the invention of the app.

The kid's convinced I can do no wrong.
Which is pretty amazing when you think about
how much wrong I actually do.

I guess you could say he sort of idolizes me.
He doesn't even get pissed
when he catches me in a lie.

He just gets this real astonished look
on that innocent little mug of his,
like he can't believe I did it again.

Then he bursts out laughing
and says, "That wath mega cool!
Tell me *another* thtory!"

I Totally Lucked Out
in the Brother Department

I mean,
Will was so psyched
to go to Paris this summer.

He had this whole plan all worked out—
he was going to climb
to the top of the Eiffel Tower

as many times as it took
for him to earn himself a spot
in the *Guinness Book of World Records*.

But when Mom told us her evil plan,
Will didn't throw a tantrum
(like *I* did).

And he didn't stomp all around the house,
slamming drawers and closet doors
(like *Mom* did while I was *throwing* my tantrum).

He just trotted over to me,
slipped his hand into mine,
then beamed his gap-toothed grin at me

and said, "I don't care where the heck
I thpend the thummer,
ath long ath I thpend it with *you*."

See what I mean?
You've got to love
a kid like that.

And I Do Love Him . . . Most of the Time

But at the moment, he's flinging
half-eaten gummy worms at me.

And he won't stop asking
if we're there yet,

and demanding to know
why we aren't there yet,

and commanding me to tell him
exactly how many more minutes

and seconds and nanoseconds
it will be till we *are* there.

I swear to God—
if that kid asks me

to play one more game
of I Spy With My Little Eye,

I'm gonna sock him one
with my little fist.

Though I Don't Blame Him for Being So Whiny

I mean, isn't it bad enough
that Mom's forcing us
to go on location with her?

Did she *really* have to pick
Friday afternoon at rush hour
to drag us there?

The traffic
is at a complete and total
standstill now.

We literally
haven't moved forward,
even one single inch, in eons.

The pressure in my head is building . . .
I feel like a nuclear reactor
getting ready to melt down . . .

I have got
to get out
of this car!

I Slip My Fingers Around
the Door Handle

And I'm just about
to make a run for it—
when the traffic clears
and our car surges forward!

Will gives me
a sticky high five
as we zoom up
the Pacific Coast Highway.

I roll down the window
and close my eyes,
letting the breeze rake its fingers
through my hair.

And for a few delicious minutes,
I'm so relieved to be moving again,
that I don't even care
where we're going.

Then

I hear the thundering rumble
of a mufflerless engine,
and turn to look over my shoulder
for the source of the racket.

Roaring up fast,
in the narrow aisle
between the lanes of cars,
is a guy on a gleaming black motorcycle.

I hate it when bikers do that—
like they think they have
their own private freeway
running right down the middle of ours.

"That guy has a death wish," Mom says.
"If I ever catch you kids on one of those,
you'll be grounded for life."
"If we don't get killed firtht!" Will chirps.

As the biker approaches,
I see that he's wearing a ridiculously cool helmet
with a pair of tinted silver-rimmed goggles
built right into it.

The goggles hide most of his face,
but the parts that I *can* see—
the tip of his nose . . . those full lips . . .
that stubbly chin . . .

make him look sort of like
a cross between Ryan Gosling,
Channing Tatum,
and a young Bradley Cooper.

A Second Later

He pulls up right next to us.
And, for some strange reason,
that's when he decides to slow down.

So now,
we're cruising along the highway,
side by side.

And then
it's like a scene straight out
of one of my mother's movies—

because the guy turns to look right *at* me
and, for a split second,
our eyes lock.

Well,
I mean, his *goggles*
and my eyes lock.

He flashes me a smile—and suddenly
I feel like I'm a pile of dry kindling
and he's a lit match.

Then he gives me this funny little salute,
guns his engine,
and vrooms out of sight.

I slump down in my seat
and try to catch my breath,
wondering if I imagined the whole thing.

Until Will says,
"Whoa . . . Death Wish Dude
thinkth you're hot!"

I Hope My Brother's Right About That

But I seriously doubt it.
It's just that the guy's probably never
seen a girl with purple eyes before.

Oh, wait.
I forgot to tell you about my eyes,
didn't I?

Yup—they're purple.
And nope—that's not just
another one of my whoppers.

My eyes really *are* purple.
At least they are *today*.
But tomorrow, who knows?

They might be pink.
Or orange.
Or neon green.

How is that possible? you ask.
Easy: I wear tinted contacts.
A different color every day.

I guess you could say
it's sort of my trademark.
That, and all my piercings.

I wear so many earrings
that I actually jingle when I walk.
It annoys the crap out of my mother.

So, yeah. Mission accomplished.

But as Far as Death Wish Dude Is Concerned

I guess it doesn't matter
one way or the other

whether he noticed my purple eyes,
or my piercings,

or if he thought I was cute
or not.

Because I'm never
going to see the guy again . . .

And I'm contemplating
this monumentally sad fact,

when I hear a thundering rumble
coming from behind us.

My eyes dart
to the rearview mirror.

And—omigod!
There he is again.

How the heck
did he get behind us . . . ?

He would have had to change lanes
and slow way down,

then wait till he saw us drive by
and switch back into *our* lane.

But why would he have bothered
going to all that trouble?

Unless . . .
  Unless . . .

    Could Will
      have been right?

Nah, the Guy Probably Spotted *Mom*

And now he's doubled back
to try to get a closer look at her.
Or I suppose it could be
a coincidence.

But, just in case,
I duck down in my seat to apply
a fresh layer of "Kiss Me Quick" gloss
while simultaneously fluffing out my bangs.

When I sit back up,
Death Wish Dude zips out from behind us and,
for the second time today, starts cruising along
right next to my open window!

He turns to flash me
another dazzling smile.
This one practically gives me
sunspots.

"*God*, that's loud," Mom says.
"Why doesn't he get a muffler for that thing?"
"A muffler would ruin the effect," Will explains.
"It would cut the coolneth factor right in half."

Maybe it's my *heart*
that needs a muffler—
it's beating so loud
I can't hear myself swoon.

Because now the guy's staring
into my eyes again.
Staring straight through his silver goggles
right into my eyes . . .

And now he's pulling
a slip of paper out of his pocket,
waving it at me
like he wants me to take it . . .

I reach out through the window,
with trembling fingers,
and somehow manage
to grab it from him.

Then he gives me
that funny little salute again,
and tears off down the road,
leaving me to eat his dust.

I look down at the paper in my hand.
And when I see the five words
that are scrawled on it,
I'm so stunned it isn't even funny:

None of this really happened.

Actually . . .

Those are *my* five words.
Not Death Wish Dude's.

Though you already knew
I was making that last part up, right?

I mean, I *did* have, like,
a "moment" with him.

But everything after page 36
was pure fabrication.

(Except for the stuff about the tinted contacts
and the piercings. That part was true.)

But the guy on the motorcycle
never came back that second time.

And he never gave me
a slip of paper.

Though, honestly—didn't you find it
even a teensy bit hard to believe

that he could somehow manage
to reach into his pocket and hand me a note,

while driving
at sixty miles an hour

down that skinny little lane
between the rows of cars,

without ending up
as a pile of steaming road kill?

You *Didn't?*

Dang, I'm good!
I think maybe that's one of the reasons
I'm so addicted to lying:

it's the only thing
I'm any good at—
my one true talent.

My shrink disagrees with that theory.
She says I lie because I've got a very bad case
of Daughter-of-a-Famous-Movie-Star Disorder.

She says I lie
to escape out from under
my mother's massive shadow.

I say I lie
because it's the most fun I can have
with my clothes on.

Not That I've Had That Much Fun
With My Clothes *Off*

Not *yet* anyway.
Though I told everyone at school
that I lost my virginity during a party,
with the son of that guy who starred in . . .

Well, it doesn't matter
who I told them I did it with.
Because it wasn't true.
I haven't done it with anyone.

But I had to lie about it.
I mean, you're considered a freak
at Lakewood High if you haven't
given it up by the time you turn fifteen.

I'll be *sixteen*
in August.
And I'm still
pitifully pure.

Though,
to tell you the truth,
I haven't actually *wanted*
to do it with anyone.

Why Haven't I Wanted to Do It With Anyone?

Because as soon as
I start going out with a guy,
it seems like it only takes about a minute
till he gets me alone and starts
ramming his tongue down my throat.

And it's only
a matter of seconds after that
till he moves on to grabbing my boobs
and squeezing them like he's trying
to juice a couple of oranges.

And, well . . .
it's weird.
Because I don't get turned on
by any of this.
I just get grossed out.

Which worries me a little.
Okay. It worries me a lot.
Because, I mean, I'm supposed
to *like* making out, aren't I?
I'm supposed to *enjoy* getting groped.

What if I'm frigid or something . . . ?

So, Yeah

My innocence
is still very much intact.

Because the boys I date
end up dumping me pretty fast

when it becomes obvious that I'm not
even interested in going to third base.

Let alone
all the way.

Though lots of guys
I've never even gone *out* with

have tried to relieve me
of my "burden"—

mostly stoned or drunk jerks
at random parties.

For some reason,
guys like that seem to think

that any girl
who isn't home in bed by midnight

might as well be wearing a sign
that says I'M ASKING FOR IT.

But I've found
that a swift knee to the nuts

goes a long way toward relieving them
of that dumbass notion.

Oh, and By the Way

Don't even think
about telling anyone
what I just told you—

all that stuff
about my still being a virgin
and everything.

I'm serious.
If you breathe a single word of that
to anyone,

I will
hunt you down.
And I will kill you.

Well,
maybe I won't actually
kill you.

But I'll spread such a hideous
(and totally convincing)
pack of lies about you,

that you'll wish I *had*.

Three Potty Breaks, Two Mini-Golf Stops, and One KFC Run Later

Mom steers her Prius
onto the long curving driveway of the hotel,
where everyone who's working on *Love Canoe*
will live during the filming.

I honestly don't know whether
to jump for joy or jump off a cliff . . .
Oh, wait. I *do* know.
I'm definitely opting for the cliff.

I mean, is she kidding me?
Ten weeks in *this* place?
It's after midnight, and dimly lit,
so I can't see the grounds that well,

but let's just say
that if Fred Flintstone and Barbie
got together to design a hotel,
it would probably look like this.

Most of the buildings seem to be
made out of these cheesy fake boulders.
And the ones that aren't have been painted
a truly scary shade of Pepto Bismol pink—

which is a shade of pink
you never *ever* see
when you
are in Paris.

We Enter the Lobby

Pink couches,
pink candelabras,
pink clouds painted all over the walls,

and a skinny guy in his twenties,
with an enormous Adam's apple,
snoring away behind the front desk.

Will gets
a dangerous gleam in his eye,
and before Mom or I can stop him,

he whacks his hand down
on the round silver bell on the counter
and shouts, "Time to wake up, thleepyhead!"

The clerk's eyes fly open.
He leaps up, still half-asleep, and yells,
"Anything but the pickle!"

This triggers a giggle fit in Will.
Then Mom starts giggling too.
And so do I.

The clerk looks around, blinking in confusion.
And when his eyes land on Mom,
he does a classic double take.

"You're . . . you're Marissa Shawn!" he gasps.
"That's right," my mother says,
glancing at his name tag. "And you're Dexter."

Then she flashes him
one of her patented smiles, and Dexter's cheeks
turn even pinker than the hotel.

When he finally manages to speak,
he says, "Let me be the first to welcome you
to the Nirvana Inn, Ms. Shawn."

Mom bats
her ludicrously long lashes at him
and coos, "Thank you, Dexter darling."

I hate it when she does that.
She calls everyone she meets "darling."
She says it makes them feel special.

And maybe it does.
But it makes *me* feel
nauseous.

Dexter Can't Take His Eyes
off Mom's Chest

"You're even
more awesome in person
than you are on film," he gushes.

Will catches my eye
and makes the universal sign
for "gag me."

Then he turns to our mother,
as innocent as anything,
and asks,

"Mommy,
why ith that man
thtaring at your boobth?"

Dexter Quickly Shifts His Gaze
to the Ceiling

Mom shoots Will
a boy-are-you-gonna-get-it look.

Dexter's Adam's apple
starts bouncing up and down,

like there's a tiny trampoline
lodged inside his neck.

But he doesn't wait
for Mom to answer Will's question.

He just launches into
a memorized spiel about the hotel:

"The Nirvana Inn has a hundred rooms.
Each one with its own unique theme."

Then he starts reeling off some names:
"Mermaid's Cove, UFO Fantasy, Dinosaur Den . . ."

Which is when
Will cries, "Mega cool!"

and announces
that he needs to see *all* the rooms

before he picks
which one he wants to stay in.

Dexter steals
an anxious glance at my mother,

then tells Will
that that's against hotel policy.

Will bites his lower lip,
trying not to cry.

But the poor kid's just too tired
to keep it together.

Mom Wipes Away His Tears

"Aw, Wilson," she says,
pulling him in for a hug.
"The rooms have people sleeping in them.
We can't wake them all up."

Then she curls
a lock of her white-blond hair
around her finger and plants another
movie-star smile on Dexter, like a kiss.

And, without taking her eyes off his,
she purrs, "I'm sure this young man
would help us if he could.
But he's just a hotel clerk.

Not Superman . . ."

And, Of Course, That's All It Takes

Moments later,
Dexter and his Adam's apple
are whisking us into
a room called Zootopia.

It's completely crazy—with zebra-print
couches, leopard-print comforters,
and real tiger-skin rugs
scattered across the floor.

"Wow!" Will cries.
"I don't need to look
at any of the other roomth.
Thith one ith perfect!"

Then he leaps onto the nearest bed,
lays his head down
on the leopard-print comforter,
and in ten seconds flat

he's snoring
even louder than Dexter was
when we first walked into
the lobby.

Dexter Sidles Over to Mom

And then the sleazoid
actually has the nerve to suggest
that the two of them leave me here
to babysit for Will, while he shows *her*
the rest of the unoccupied rooms.

"No thanks," Mom says.
Dexter looks as deflated
as an old birthday balloon.
Even his Adam's apple looks dejected.
But Mom doesn't seem to notice.

She just asks him
to unlock the doors to the rooms
that connect on either side of Will's,
hands him a twenty-dollar bill,
and sends him to get our luggage.

Then,
in a rare instance of selflessness,
she tells me
that I can take my pick
between the two rooms.

On one side, is Sweet Suite—
the tackiest place imaginable,
with cupcake lampshades,
ice-cream cone wallpaper,
and jelly bean bedspreads.

On the other side, is Love Shack—
a room positively crawling with golden cupids,
that has this clunky winding staircase
leading up to a dumb little tower
with heart-shaped stained glass windows.

The tower
makes me think of Rapunzel—
how she was trapped with no way out.
Which is a situation
I can definitely relate to.

So I figure I might as well choose this one.

I Flop Down Onto the Bed

And that's when I realize
how blue the walls are.

And how blue the bedspread is . . .
and the rug is . . .

This room is way too blue.
But *I'm* even bluer.

I mean, I can't believe I'll be stuck
in this dump all summer.

I squeeze my eyes closed,
fighting back tears.

Then, a distant roll of thunder
floats in through the window . . .

Or maybe it's the sound
of a wave breaking on the beach . . .

Or—
omigod!

Could it be the rumbling
of an unmuffled engine?

I Sprint Up the Stairway to the Tower

And fling open one of the windows.
There, zooming up the winding driveway,
is Death Wish Dude!

He pulls over near the front of the hotel,
climbs down from his motorcycle,
and lifts off his helmet.

Then he turns and looks in my direction.
And when his eyes find mine,
a huge grin spreads across his face—

this gorgeous
glinty-toothed
pirate-y sort of grin.

And I have no idea
how he found out
where I'm staying.

But I don't *care*
how he found out.
I'm just glad he did.

I suck in a breath,
then gesture for him
to come up to my room.

And when he lifts his chin at me,
and heads toward the hotel entrance,
my heart practically leaps out of my chest.

Or at Least It *Would* Have Leaped
Out of My Chest

If Death Wish Dude
had actually shown up.

But the truth is,
that last part wasn't exactly true.

Okay.
It wasn't even slightly true.

Death Wish Dude
didn't come to my hotel.

Though it sure was fun
imagining that he *did*, wasn't it?

Are you starting to see, now,
why I'm so addicted

to reinventing
reality?

Saturday (Day #1 in Hell)

Mom wakes Will and me at noon,
then drags us downstairs and asks Sid,
the chauffeur DreamWorks hired for her,

to drive the three of us
to downtown San Luis Obispo,
so we can check it out.

It's easy to see why
they call this place SLO.
There is less than zero going on here.

The upside to this is
that there are no paparazzi following us around
like packs of starving wolves.

The downside is that the SLOians
are so starved for excitement
that they swarm around Mom like mosquitoes,

hounding her for autographs
whenever she stands still too long
in any one spot.

And, I mean, where will I shop all summer?
There's no Betsey Johnson, no Marc Jacobs.
There's not even a Bloomingdale's!

And there's nothing to eat either—
no In-N-Out Burger, no Poquito Mas . . .
No nothing.

Just a few
crummy coffee shops
full of aging hippies,

plus a dinky little art museum,
a dinky little history museum,
a dinky little mission,

and, last but definitely least—
a prehistoric movie theater
that only shows *one* film.

Help!
I'm trapped in the armpit
of the universe!

When We Get Back to the Hotel

Mom says she's going to take a little nap,
and promises that when she wakes up,
she'll take Will and me to Shangri-la—
the fancy steakhouse at the hotel.

But then Jack Dane
(Mom's *Love Canoe* costar)
calls to ask her to have dinner with *him*.
So, naturally, she ditches us.

When I see how bummed Will is,
I decide to take him
to Shangri-la myself.
Which is where we are right now—

a restaurant so drenched in pink
that it's like sitting on the back
of a flamingo. At sunset.
Wearing rose-tinted sunglasses.

During dinner, I point out
three Russian spies who are eyeing us
suspiciously from across the room.
Will slides closer to me in our booth.

Then I point out two space aliens,
disguised as a pair of harmless old ladies,
scanning the restaurant for earthlings to abduct.
Will inches even closer to me.

"And see that fat guy
at the table right next to us?" I whisper.
"The guy who keepth on looking at me?"
Will whispers back.

"Yeah," I say. "That's Cannibal Man.
He escaped from a freak show today
and he's famous for eating . . .
seven-year-old boys!"

Then I grab Will
and pretend to chomp on his arm.
"I know you're making all thith up," he giggles.
"Tho why am I thtill tho thcared?"

"Because," I say,
taking another bite out of his arm,
"I'm the world's best liar."
"Damn thtraight!" Will says.

When the Waitress Asks Us
If We Want Dessert

I take her aside to whisper in her ear,
while Will fiddles with a sugar packet,
pretending not to see us.

Then, a few minutes later,
she brings him a gigantic slice of fudge cake
with a candle stuck in it.

Will thanks her,
sneaks me a secret thumbs-up,
then blows out the candle.

Though,
as you might have guessed,
it's *not* Will's birthday.

We're
just pulling
our "free dessert" scam—

the one we *always* pull
whenever the two of us
go out to eat.

After Dinner

Will and I snuggle together
under his leopard-print comforter,
while I tell him a bedtime story.

I love making up stories for him.
And this one is kind of inspired,
if I do say so myself.

It's about this seven-year-old orphan boy
who sneaks into the zoo and ends up
getting adopted by a family of monkeys.

Will's hanging on my every word.
Though he interrupts me now and then
to ask when Mom will be back.

Finally, he drifts off to sleep,
and I jot down some notes about
my orphan story on some hotel stationery.

Because, I mean, you never know—
some detail in it might come in handy
someday for one of my lies.

Then I try texting
Crystal, Bette, and Madison.
But no one texts me back.

Not even when I tell them I'm having
a torrid affair with the director's son
and offer to tell them all the juicy details.

I guess they don't believe me.
Or maybe they're still mad
about Paris . . .

Oh, Who Am I Kidding?

They're definitely still mad about Paris.
I don't think they'll *ever* forgive me
for canceling our trip.

My throat clamps shut
when I think about how they reacted
when I told them.

Crystal said, "You never had any
intention of taking us to Paris, did you?
It was just more of your usual BS."

Bette said, "You lying little freak . . .
I can't believe all three of us fell
for another one of your hideous cons."

And Madison said . . .
Well . . . she said
a whole bunch of things.

But I don't
really feel like
repeating them here.

I Close My Eyes

Then I wrap my arms around Will,
trying to let his snoring drown out
the memory of their acid words . . .

And the next thing I know,
Mom's waking us both up
to apologize for ditching us.

I glance at the clock—
it's after two a.m.
That must have been *some* "dinner" . . .

She's slurring her words a little,
promising that tomorrow
she'll spend the whole day with us.

"Thas why I brought you up here," she says.
"So the three of us could have fun together
when I wasn't busy shooting."

She says we'll find
the nearest beach
and go surfing and boogie boarding.

Then we'll look
for one of those moon-bounce things
Will loves so much.

And after lunch,
we'll leave him with a sitter, so we girls
can get mani-pedis at the hotel spa.

If Mom
keeps her promise,
tomorrow might actually be fun.

But I'm not gonna hold my breath.

Sunday (Day #2 in Hell)

Will and I tried to wake Mom up at ten.
But she just pulled the pillow
over her head and moaned,
"I need my beauty sleep . . ."

So we ordered room service
(runny eggs and cold toast)
and spent the next few hours
watching *Spiderman 12* or whatever.

And then, at two o'clock,
when we finally managed
to drag Mom out of bed,
and were just about to head to the beach,

Jack called
to invite her to have a drink
and "go over the scenes"
they'll be shooting tomorrow.

So,
of course,
she accepted his offer.
Big shock, right?

Before she left, she promised us
she'd be back in time for dinner.
But six o'clock rolled around.
And then seven.

Now, it's eight o'clock.
And Will and I
are dining on room service again
(greasy fries and soggy chicken fingers).

Our mother makes a *lot* of promises.

Monday (Day #3 in Hell)

Mom's been on the set all day.
And I've been babysitting Will.

She offered to hire
a professional sitter for him.

But Will got all weepy about it.
So I told Mom *I'd* look after him.

It's not like I've got anyone *else*
to hang out with, right?

Though now,
I'm having second thoughts.

I mean, I love my brother.
Really, I do.

But playing a zillion games of Uno
and Candy Land gets old pretty fast.

Tuesday (Day #4 in Hell)

See:
"Monday (Day #3 in Hell)."

Only instead of playing
a zillion games of Uno and Candy Land,

we play a zillion games of
Connect 4 and Chutes and Ladders.

Wednesday (Day #5 in Hell)

See:
"Tuesday (Day #4 in Hell)."

Only instead of playing a zillion games
of Connect 4 and Chutes and Ladders,

we play a zillion games of Battleship
and Hungry Hungry Totally Annoying Hippos.

Thursday (Day #6 in Hell)

This
is getting
ridiculous.

Do you realize
how many more days it'll be
till they're finished filming *Love Canoe*?

58!
How am I possibly
going to survive that long?

Mom's been working all day,
then rushing off every night,
to "run through her lines" with Jack.

(I don't know why she doesn't
just admit she's screwing him.
She *always* has a thing with her costar.)

But at least today is Thursday.
Which means that tonight's the night—
the night of the "big event."

The most exciting event of the SLO week.
The *only* event of the SLO week:
the farmers' market.

I Thought It Would Be Just as Slow as the Rest of SLO

In fact, I almost refused to get out of the limo
when Sid dropped Will and me off
and said he'd pick us back up at nine.

Man . . .
three hours wandering around
staring at a bunch of fruits and vegetables?

It doesn't
get much lamer
than that.

Though now that we're actually here . . .
Well, I hate to admit this . . .
But it's sort of . . . well . . . fun—

almost like being at a huge block party
where you don't really know anyone,
but everyone's super friendly.

And, I mean, there *are*
a thousand booths selling fruits
and vegetables and stuff.

But there's also
magicians and jugglers
and musicians jamming on every corner.

And the food?
Unbefreakinglievable.
Spicy chili bubbling in vats,

fresh corn roasting in its husks,
and, everywhere, the smoky-sweet smell
of barbecue hissing on grills . . .

Will and I Pigged Out on Pork Ribs

Which made us ridiculously thirsty.
So we guzzled enormous glasses
of the best lemonade on planet Earth.

And now—
both of us have to pee.
Desperately.

We zip over to the park
to use the facilities near the corner
where Sid dropped us off.

But when I try to yank Will
into the ladies' room with me,
he digs his heels into the dirt.

"Colette," he says, "I'm theven yearth old!"
"And your point is . . . ?"
"I'm too old for the girlth room."

My bladder
is getting ready to burst.
I don't have time to argue.

I shove him into the men's room,
begging him to hurry,
and wait for him right outside the door.

By the time he trots back out,
I've concocted a lie to try to scare him
into joining me in the ladies' room.

"The police just came by to warn everyone
that a lion's escaped from the circus!" I say.
"So you better come inside with me."

"No thankth," he says with a grin.
"But if the lion comth by and he'th hungry,
I'll thend him in to eat *you*."

"Don't be such a comedian," I say,
sitting him down on a nearby bench.
"And don't budge from this spot!"

Then I Turn and Race
Into the Bathroom

When I reach out
to grab the handle of the stall
I see some graffiti on the door—

"Hello!" some SLOian has written
in these real friendly curly letters.
"Got to go wee wee?"

"I sure do," I say,
laughing to myself
as I sprint into the stall.

A minute later, while I'm washing my hands,
I glance in the mirror and wonder
if maybe I should change my look,

maybe try streaking my hair
with pink and purple and orange
to match my various contact lenses . . .

And that's when I notice still more graffiti—
scrawled across the top of the mirror:
"Change how you see. Not how you look."

Well, what do you know?
I think to myself.
A psychic mirror . . .

And I'm still giggling
at the thought of this,
when all of a sudden it dawns on me

that I've forgotten
about my brother—
sitting outside on that bench

all
by
himself.

I Shove Open the Door

And my heart freezes
in mid-beat—

the bench
where I left Will,

the bench
that I told him not to budge from,

is totally and completely
and terrifyingly

empty!

I Can't Breathe

There's a ringing in my ears.
I feel like I might faint.

Or barf.
Or both.

I start dashing all over the place,
calling his name again and again . . .

Searching
behind bushes . . .

behind trees . . .
in trees . . .

down by the creek . . .
under the bridge . . .

Asking everyone in my path
if they've seen him . . .

Running . . . running . . .
turning in circles . . .

my throat so tight now
I can barely call his name . . .

What Was I *Thinking*?

I can't believe I left you alone.
How could I have been such an idiot?

Don't be gone, Will . . .
Please . . . don't be gone . . .

I swear to God,
if you're alive when I find you,

I am totally
going to kill you!

Will! *Will!*
WILL! *WILL!*

Where the hell *are* you?

Then—

I hear:
"Thith ith mega cool . . ."

It's coming from behind me.
I whip around.

And there he is—
across the park!

But
oh *no* . . .

He's climbing up onto a motorcycle
behind some perv!

I charge toward them
like a raging bull.

If that pedophile
tries to ride off with my brother

he'll have to
mow me down first.

A Second Later, I Reach Will's Side

"You weren't supposed
to leave that bench," I say,
yanking him off the motorcycle
and pulling him in for a bone-crushing hug.

I squeeze my eyes closed,
inhale his gummy-worm scent,
feel his skinny arms
hugging me back.

"I couldn't find you . . . ,"
I murmur into his corn-silk hair.
"I was so worried."
"I'm thorry," Will whispers.

"But I thought that lion thtory
wath another one of your fibth.
Tho I figured it would be thafe
to look around a little."

"It's all my fault," I say,
squeezing him even tighter.
"I should have warned you
not to talk to strangers."

"Oh, but he'th not a thtranger," Will says.
Which is when I open my eyes
to peer, for the first time,
at the motorcycle's owner.

And—
omigod . . .
That's no pedophile.
That's Death Wish Dude!

Or . . .

Wait!
Maybe
Death Wish Dude
is a pedophile . . .

Maybe it wasn't me *or* Mom
he was smiling at
when he pulled up
next to our car that day.

Maybe he was smiling
at my *brother*!
Will squirms out of our hug
and I take a step back on wobbly legs.

The guy hops off his bike
and slips his hands
into the pockets
of his vintage leather jacket.

He's wearing that helmet
with the built-in goggles.
So I still can't see his eyes.
But I can see that smile of his.

And it is definitely not
the smile of a pedophile.
Though it seems to be putting me
under some kind of spell or something.

Because,
I know this sounds crazy,
but I feel seriously bewitched right now.
Or bewarlocked, or whatever.

Like if this guy snaps his fingers,
I'll do whatever he tells me to do . . .
Even if he asks me to slip my T-shirt off
over my head and—

A Tug on My Sleeve Wakes Me From My Daydream

Will's beaming up at me
with a proud gap-toothed grin,

gesturing toward Death Wish Dude,
saying,

"Colette, allow me to introduthe Connor.
Connor, thith ith Colette."

"Hey . . . ," I manage to croak,
my mouth suddenly gone insanely dry.

"Hey, Colette . . . ," Connor says,
lifting his chin in greeting.

Whoa . . .
His voice . . .

So husky and low,
just a cut above a whisper . . .

And now he's saying my name again,
rolling it over his tongue

like he's savoring a lick
of an ice-cream cone.

"Colette . . . ," he murmurs.
"It's the perfect name for you."

And when he says this,
a shiver runs through me—

because it feels like
he's undressing me

with his words.

Then, Without Warning

Connor reaches up,
whipping off his helmet
and goggles.

And my heart
literally skips a beat.
Like: beat, beat, ——, beat.

His hair!
It's so awesome
it isn't even funny—

cropped close to his head,
and dyed to look like tiger skin,
with alternating stripes of orange and black.

And his eyes!
The most incredible shade of amber gold . . .
Melting into mine . . .

"Man . . . ," he says,
flashing me a dizzying smile.
"You've got amazing eyes."

"*I've* got amazing eyes?"
"Yeah," he says, "I've never seen
a girl with purple eyes before."

I've been so entranced by *his* eyes,
(and his hair and his voice and his smile)
that I forgot I was wearing contacts.

But,
now that he's reminded me,
I just shrug and say,

"Genetics."

I Glance Over at Will

He's gaping at Connor,
his eyes as big as DVDs.
"Were you *born* with that hair?" he asks.

"Nope," Connor says. "I dyed it."
"Well, it'th unbelievable," Will says.
"It lookth jutht like the rugth in my room."

"Let me guess," Connor says.
"You're stayin' in Zootopia,
over at the Nirvana Inn."

Will and I
practically keel over.
"How did you know *that*?" I say.

"Oh, we locals know that place
like the backs of our hands," he says,
running his fingers over his hair.

And *my* fingers tingle,
imagining the furry softness
of it . . .

Then he says, "Sorry I scared you before.
I wasn't gonna kidnap your brother.
Though he *is* a pretty cute kid."

"I thertainly am!" Will says,
puffing out his scrawny little chest.
And Connor and I exchange a smile.

"That's okay," I tell Connor.
"It's not like I thought you were
a pedophile or anything."

Which is when
Will turns to him and asks,
"What'th a pedophile?"

Connor opens his mouth to speak,
but no words come out.
He darts me a nervous glance.

"Oh, you don't have to answer that," I say.
"Asking embarrassing questions
is my brother's hobby."

Connor laughs—
a deep, throaty laugh.
And the sound of it

vibrates all through me . . .
like I'm a wind chime
and he's

the breeze.

Will Grins Up at Connor and Me

"Athking embarrathing quethtionth
ith not my hobby," he says.
"It'th jutht thumthing I enjoy doing
in my thpare time."

Connor and I share a laugh at this.
"Now that you two are friendth," Will says,
"can I thit on your bike
and pretend I'm driving?"

"It's all right with me," Connor says,
"if it's all right with your sister."
"Why not?" I say,
helping Will back onto the seat.

Will winks at me and says,
"What Mom duthn't know
won't hurt me, right?"
"Exactly right," I say.

If Will
had a tail,
it would definitely
be wagging right now.

"Do you want
to get up there with him?" Connor asks,
offering me his hand for a boost up.
And I'm just about to take hold of it,

when I hear a loud horn honking.

I Look Across the Park and See Sid

He's waving us over to the limo.
Damn!
It must be nine o'clock.

I feel like Cinderella—forced to leave the ball
after just one dance with the prince,
before my coach turns into a pumpkin.

"Thid'th here *already*?" Will grumbles.
"Sid's a friend of our mom's," I tell Connor.
"He drives a limo."

Will shoots me a look
as he climbs back down off the bike,
but he doesn't reveal my lie.

"Then I guess you've got to go . . . ," Connor says.
"Yeah, I guess . . . ," I say.
"Thith totally thuckth," Will says.

Connor laughs and says, "It totally *does*, dude."
Then he turns to me, searching my eyes
like he's hunting for buried treasure.

Finally, he says, "You don't happen to have,
like, a glass slipper you could leave behind.
Or a flip flop or anything, do you?"

Wow . . .
Talk about being on the same wavelength!
This is ridiculous . . .

Will rolls his eyes.
"If you want her phone number,
why don't you jutht athk her for it?"

I'm not sure whether
I want to strangle my brother,
or get down on my knees and thank him.

Connor blushes,
in a devastatingly gorgeous way, and says,
"Maybe she doesn't *want* to give it to me . . ."

But, before I can stop myself,
I blurt out "310-555-8790."
And now it's *my* turn to blush.

Only I know from experience
that I do *not* blush
in a devastatingly gorgeous way.

I blush in a disgustingly blotchy way.
I can't let him see me like this!
"Later, 'gator . . . ," I say (like a totally lame loser).

But Connor doesn't seem
to have noticed my blotchiness.
Or even to have heard my lame remark.

He's just standing here gazing at me
like he's never seen anyone
more beautiful in his whole entire life.

And then, he takes a step closer to me,
wraps his arms around my waist,
and pulls me to him,

till our mouths
are only an inch apart.
And then . . .

then . . .

Aw, Come On

You didn't really think
he was gonna kiss me, did you?
I mean, we only met a few minutes ago.

And did you honestly believe
he wrapped his arms around me
and pulled me close?

I wish!
All he did was smile at me
and give me that funny little salute of his.

Then I grabbed Will's hand
and started pulling him across the courtyard
toward the limo.

And just before we climbed into it,
I glanced back over my shoulder
for one last peek at Connor.

But he
and his motorcycle
had vanished—

like they were just some kind of mirage . . .

The Longest Week
in the History of Weeks

Friday—
Connor doesn't call.

Saturday—
Connor doesn't call.

Sunday—
Connor doesn't call.

Monday,
Tuesday, Wednesday—

Connor doesn't call
and doesn't call and doesn't call.

I rub rabbit's feet.
I pick up lucky pennies.

I knock on wood.
I wish on stars.

I make sure I'm never more
than an arm's length away from my phone,

even when I'm splashing
in the hotel pool with Will.

And every night I fall asleep
with it tucked under my pillow,

while the golden cupids
hanging from my ceiling

look on,
wringing their chubby hands.

It's Five Thirty on Thursday Afternoon

And Will's
down on his bony little knees,
pleading with me to take him
to the farmers' market.

"Pleeeeeeeeath," he says.
"Mom'th shooting late again tonight.
Tho if *you* don't take me, I can't go.
Don't you remember how great it wath?"

I tell him I do remember,
but that I can't risk running into Connor
because I'd die of embarrassment
if he thought I was stalking him.

"*Girlth* . . . ," Will mutters under his breath.
He gets up from his knees, dusts himself off,
tugs on a wispy lock of his hair,
then launches a new attack:

"If we run into that poophead,
you can act like you don't even remember him,
which will make him feel like
he'th the thcum of the earth and then—"

Suddenly, my phone's ringing!

I Jam My Hands Into My Purse

And start
clawing through the chaos.

Don't hang up, Connor . . .
Please . . . Don't hang up!

I rummage madly through the jumble
of pens and lipsticks and hairbrushes,

but I can't find
the freaking phone!

Finally, Will yanks my purse away from me,
and empties it onto the bed.

There, amidst the rubble,
lies my cell—

glowing, pulsing,
daring me to answer it . . .

But I'm too flustered to move a muscle.
So Will grabs it and shoves it into my hands.

And when I check the caller ID,
tears sting my eyes.

Because it's not Connor.
It's Mom.

I Pick Up

"Hey, Mom," I say, trying to sound cheery.
"What's wrong?" she asks.

That is so annoying.
"Nothing is wrong," I say.

"Do you want to talk about it, Collie?"
"No! And don't call me Collie. I'm not a dog."

Though maybe I am . . . I *definitely* am . . .
That must be why Connor never called . . .

Mom knows I hate that nickname.
But she doesn't apologize for using it.

She just says, "We wrapped early today.
So I'm coming back to the hotel

to pick you and Wilson up
and take you to the farmers' market."

I tell her that they'll have to go
without me.

I tell her
my stomach hurts.

I tell her I've got a headache, too.
An über headache.

Plus a bad sore throat.
And at least *that* part's true—

it hurts to swallow when you've got
a massive lump of misery stuck in your neck.

Mom and Will Have Been Gone for a Couple of Hours

It was easy convincing her that I wasn't
BS-ing her about being under the weather.

I just used
my usual foolproof trick:

smudged a little mascara under my eyes
to make myself look sick.

Then, as soon as they left,
I drew myself a hot bubble bath.

And that's where I've been
ever since,

just lying here listening to the tiny *pop!*
each lonely bubble makes as it dissolves—

along with the last drop of hope
that Connor will ever call me.

The glow of my orange-blossom candle
throws gloomy shadows onto the wall.

My silent phone watches me
from its throne on the toilet-seat lid.

I don't know why I even bothered
bringing it into the bathroom with me.

Connor's never going to call.
Why can't I just accept that fact?

And why can't I forget
those amber eyes of his?

And that
tiger-striped hair?

Why can't I stop hearing
the echo of his laugh and his—

Whoa.
It's ringing!

I Check the Caller ID

It's him!
No, really. It *is*.
I swear to God.

I force myself
to let it ring three times
before I answer.

Then I pick up the call.
And in the most nonchalant voice ever,
I say, "Hey, Connor."

"Hey, Colette," he says.
And the flame of the candle
seems to leap.

"I've been thinkin' about you . . . ," he says.
(A guy like this doesn't need to bother with *G*s.)
"*Have* you . . . ?" I say.

I'm talking to Connor.
I'm talking to Connor
and I'm *stark naked*!

This
is the sexiest thing
that's ever happened to me . . .

"Yeah," Connor says, "I've been thinkin'
I'd like to take you for a ride.
You up for it?"

I force myself
to wait a few seconds before answering.
Then I say, as casual as anything,

"Okay. Sure. I guess so."

He'll Be Here in Twenty Minutes!

I leap out of the tub,
towel myself off,
clip my hair into an updo,
pop out my aqua contacts,
pop in my purple ones,
put on some earrings
(four of my dangliest pairs),
slather on some "Kiss Me Quick,"
slip into my slinkiest jeans,
pull on a lacy black tee,
scrawl two *went to bed early* notes,
tape one to the door of my room,
tape the other to the door
that connects to Will's,
lock the connecting door,
tiptoe into the hall,
slink down to the lobby,
and slither past Dexter,
who's dozing behind the front desk.

I Step Outside

But I stay hidden behind a bush
until I hear Connor's bike
vrooming up the driveway.

Then, I peek out to make sure Mom and Will
haven't picked this exact instant
to return from the farmers' market.

Because if Mom saw me
getting onto a motorcycle
she'd put me under permanent house arrest.

Finally, when I'm sure the coast is clear,
I step out of the shadows,
and smile at the boy of my dreams.

He smiles back,
and the butterflies in my stomach
flutter up into my throat.

Without a word,
I slip on the helmet he hands me,
climb up behind him,

wrap my arms around his waist,
and rest my cheek against
the oh-so-smooth leather of his vintage jacket.

On the Way to Morro Bay

The roar of Connor's bike
is too loud for conversation,

so we don't even try
to talk.

I just grip his thighs
with mine,

and let the throb
of the engine's motor

flow
through him

into
me . . .

And at every red light,
he takes his hand off the handle bar

and rests it, lightly,
on my knee.

This
is the sexiest thing

that's ever
happened to me.

On the Beach

Connor and I
are lying on our backs
next to each other on the sand,

our arms crossed behind our heads,
gazing up at a sky so full of stars
it almost hurts.

We've been here for a while now,
not saying much, just listening to the waves
lap and lick and shush against the shore.

Our hands are so close, only a few inches apart.
It'd be so easy to let my fingers drift over
and brush against his . . .

And man, just *thinking* about doing that
makes me feel like a wildfire's
whooshing through my veins . . .

A scorching shiver runs through me.
Connor notices and says, "You cold?"
"Yeah," I say. "Freezing."

I sit up and Connor sits up too.
He shrugs off his leather jacket
and drapes it over my shoulders.

If he was like any other guy,
he'd use this move as an excuse
to sneak his arm around me.

But Connor's
not like any other guy.
He hasn't even tried to kiss me yet.

And,
I swear to God,
it's *killing* me.

I Slip My Arms Into the Sleeves of His Jacket

Just breathing in
its leathery Connory scent
almost makes me tipsy.

Then he shifts his position, and I do too,
till we're facing each other, sitting cross-legged,
our knees dangerously close to touching.

"Warmer now?" he asks.
"Much," I say,
and that's no lie.

"I like all your earrings," he says. "So . . . dangly."
"I like all your stripes," I say. "So . . . tigery."
And we share a shy smile.

Then,
Connor picks up a handful of sand,
and lets it sift through his fingers.

I reach out,
cup my hands below his,
and catch the sand as it falls,

wishing that cradling its night-cooled softness
could somehow make time,
make this moment, stand still.

Then, I let the grains trickle through *my* fingers,
and Connor cups his hands beneath mine
to catch the sifted streams.

He lets it drift though his fingers again,
and while it's falling into my cupped hands,
he smiles at me and says,

"Wouldn't it be great
if doin' this could somehow
make time stop?"

Gulp . . . There's that wavelength thing again . . .

Connor Peers Into My Eyes
for a Minute

Then he says, "You were thinkin'
the same thing, weren't you?"

"Yeah . . . ," I admit.
"Sorta."

"You and me," he says. "We're on, like,
this weird shared wavelength."

Yikes.
There it is *again*.

I waggle my eyebrows at him and say,
"We're even on the same wavelength . . ."

And then, together, we say,
". . . about being on the same wavelength."

Which cracks us both up.
But then I'm seized by a wave of panic.

"You're not, like, a mind reader
or anything, are you?"

"I don't think so," he says.
"Though maybe we should test it out."

He rubs his hand, very deliberately,
over his tiger-striped head, and says,

"Okay: Your favorite colors
are . . . orange and black. Am I right?"

"You wish," I say.
And we crack up again.

Suddenly

We're talking—
about everything and about nothing

and about all the stuff
in between.

Connor tells me he's eighteen,
so I tell him I am too,

because if he knew I was only fifteen,
he probably wouldn't want to see me anymore.

He asks me how I like San Luis Obispo,
and I don't want to insult his hometown,

so I tell him I love
how quiet and low-key it is.

Then he asks me
what brought me here.

But there's no way I'm gonna reveal
who my mother is . . .

A million lies whirl through my brain
before I finally come up with the perfect one:

"My mother's Marissa Shawn's stand-in,
on that film that just started shooting here."

"That makes sense."
"It does?"

"Yeah.
You look like you could be Shawn's daughter.

Only you're much prettier
than she is."

"In your dreams," I say.
"You *have* been . . . ," he says.

". . . Every night since I first saw you
through the window of your car."

And Then

He reaches for my hands,
and we weave our fingers,

lacing them,
and unlacing them,

over
and over again,

sometimes pressing our palms together,
like we're high-fiving in slow motion,

sometimes pressing
all ten of our fingertips together,

as if we're touching
the face of a mirror.

Sometimes Connor writes things
onto my palm with his forefinger.

Things like:
Y-O-U + M-E,

his touch so delicate,
so delicious

that it sends thrilling currents
zooming all through me—

the kind of currents
that, until now,

I've only read about
in books . . .

This is the sexiest thing
that's ever happened to me.

I Look Up Into His Face

Then, very slowly,
we both start leaning in,

bringing our mouths closer . . .
and closer still . . .

And just as our lips
are about to touch,

a rogue wave
slams onto the shore.

Connor and I leap up, grab our helmets,
and scramble away from the rushing water.

We're fast,
but not fast enough—

our sneakers and the legs of our jeans
are soaked.

"Shit! Shit! Shit!" we shout in unison.
Then we both start laughing.

Our eyes connect for a split second.
But our starlight mood's been obliterated

by the ocean's
cold shower.

And Even Though
I'm Freezing to Death

When Connor takes hold of my hand
and says, "Come on. I better get you home.
Don't want you catchin' pneumonia . . ."

every cell
in my body
seems to catch fire.

But an instant later,
as if the universe wants to make
absolutely positively 100 percent sure

that Connor and I will not,
under any circumstances,
kiss each other tonight—

my phone starts ringing.

It's Will Calling

"That note that you left on the door
thaid you went to thleep early.
But you jutht anthered your phone,
tho I gueth you're *not* athleep."

His voice sounds a little bit wobbly—
like he's trying not to cry.
"Good guess," I say. "So, what's up, Will?
Is something the matter?"

"No . . . But Mom went out
and left me here in my room all by mythelf.
She told me you'd be right nextht door
if there were any emergenthies.

But I jutht *had* an emergenthy, and when
I knocked on your door you didn't open it."
My heart punches up into my throat
like a big guilty fist.

"What kind of emergency, kiddo?"
"The kind of emergenthy
where I thtart worrying
that you *aren't* right nextht door

and that maybe I'm completely alone here
and that if there *were* an emergenthy,
like an earthquake or a fire or anything,
I might be really really really thcared."

God.
Why does my chest
feel so tight all of a sudden—
like there's not enough room for my lungs?

"You know what *I* think?" Will continues.
"I think you're *not* right nextht door."
"You are doing some excellent thinking," I say,
trying to put a positive spin on it.

"I think," Will says,
"that you're out with Connor."
"You're amazing!" I tell him. "You're, like,
the Amazing Psychic Brother."

I hear a choked little laugh.
"But, don't worry.
I'll be home in fifteen minutes.
And I promise you

that between now and then
there won't be any earthquakes or fires."
"There better not be," he says,
in a trembly voice,

"or your ath will be grath."

On the Way Home

I've got twelve long
bone-chilling wind-whipped miles
to contemplate how strange
(and sad) it is

that the very same thing
that felt so incredibly awesome
on the over way here
(my thighs gripping Connor's thighs)

feels so incredibly *awful* now—
like my legs are encased
in a gritty crust
of frozen Play-Doh.

This
is the *un*-sexiest thing
that's ever happened
to me.

By the Time We Pull Up
in Front of the Hotel

My teeth are chattering
and I can't feel my toes.
I climb off the motorcycle,
pull off my helmet,

hand it to Connor, and say,
"Thanks for a . . . mostly great time."
He grins at me,
and I instantly begin to thaw.

"When can I see you again?" he says.
My heart does a crazy little cartwheel.
"I don't know . . .
When do you *want* to see me?"

"How about tomorrow morning," he says,
"for breakfast?"
And the eagerness in his voice
sets my whole body buzzing.

"Will there be . . . bacon involved?" I say.
"Buckets of it," he says.
"We'll order bacon with a side of bacon,
plus a couple of sides of bacon."

"You had me at 'buckets,'" I say.
Then a terrible thought hits me.
"Wait. I can't go.
I have to babysit my brother."

Connor's face clouds over.
But a split second later
he smiles and says, "No problem.
We'll bring him with us."

Then
he gives me
that funny little salute of his
and roars off into the night.

Breakfast

Sid drops Will and me off
at Louisa's Place,
the classic diner in downtown SLO
where Connor texted us to meet him.

When we walk in
and I see him sitting there,
all tiger-striped and amber-eyed,
smiling at me from that curved red booth,

my whole body starts tingling—
my thigh
will be touching *his* thigh
a second from now!

But then Will dashes ahead of me
and slips in beside Connor before I can get there,
sticking himself between the two of us
like an innocent little splinter.

I'm too embarrassed
to ask Will to switch seats with me,
so while he slurps down
cup after bottomless cup of hot cocoa,

and the three of us gorge
on bacon-stuffed waffles
with a zillion sides
of smoky-sweet bacon,

Connor and I
are reduced to exchanging
I-wish-we-were-sitting-
next-to-each-other looks.

How weird
to feel so full
and yet so hungry
at the same time . . .

After Breakfast

Will starts
bouncing up and down in the booth
like a jack-in-the-box gone berserk—

over-amped
from all the sugar
in the cocoa he just guzzled.

Then he turns to me
and asks in a stage whisper,
"Haven't you forgotten thumthing?"

"What . . . ?" I say. "Did I miss a crumb?"
"No," Will says. "But aren't you gonna
tell the waitreth it'th my birthday?"

"Oh . . . *that* . . . ," I say.
I bite my lower lip,
and steal a glance at Connor.

His face is all lit up.
"Why didn't you tell me, dude?
Happy birthday! How old are you today?"

I try to catch Will's eye—to warn him
not to let Connor in on our scheme.
But I'm too late:

"Oh, it'th not really my birthday," he says.
"It'th jutht a little thcam that Colette and I
like to pull to get a free dethert."

I look down at my lap,
afraid of what I'll find in Connor's face
if I look up.

But when I finally sneak a peek at him,
I see that he's grinning at us.
And I'm so relieved it isn't even funny.

"You guys are quite the con artists," he says.
"Yeah," Will says, high-fiving me.
"We thertainly are!"

When We're Done Sharing Will's Free Cake

Connor ushers us out of the restaurant,
and holds open the door for me—
which I've got to admit is sort of adorable
in an old-school kind of way.

"Are you gonna take uth
on a motorthycle ride now?" Will asks.
"Three people won't fit," Connor says.
"So I brought my car instead."

And he points to the Cadillac
that's parked right out front:
an antique cherry-red convertible
in mint condition.

"Thweeeet wheeeelth!" Will cries.
And he's right—this thing's
just as hot as Connor's bike.
If such a thing is even possible.

Connor holds the door open for me
and I slide onto the sun-warmed leather seat.
Will hops into the backseat.
And when we glide away from the curb,

it feels like the road's made of silk.

We Spend the Rest of the Morning

Taking Connor's tour of downtown SLO.
And we have such a blast,
it's hard to believe it's even the same town we
explored with Mom a couple of weeks ago.

First,
he takes us to Powell's Sweet Shoppe,
where he buys gummy worms for Will,
plus a huge bag of gum balls.

Then,
he leads us down the street
to show us
Bubblegum Alley—

this mondo-bizarro place
where, for decades, people have been using
big old chewed-up wads of bubblegum
to make graffiti.

There are bubblegum peace signs,
bubblegum smiley faces,
bubblegum initials
inside bubblegum hearts . . .

Will wanders through
with his mouth hanging open.
"Whoa . . . ," he says. "I've never theen
thith many germth in one plathe before!"

Connor and I crack up at this,
and he reaches for my hand.
But just before our fingers touch,
Will takes a flying leap,

grabs hold of both our hands with his,
and starts swinging back and forth
between us
like a crazed little monkey.

The anti-Cupid strikes again.

For the Next Half Hour

Connor and I chew up dozens of gum balls,
to help Will leave *his* mark
on Bubblegum Alley:

a sign that says
WILL WATH HERE.
Which Will thinks is hilarious.

And Connor and I
sort of do too,
actually.

After that, Connor takes us
to this funny novelty store
called KwirkWorld,

and buys "un-birthday presents" for us—
a pair of bacon-shaped earrings for me,
and an electronic fart machine for Will.

Then he takes us to the creek
to teach Will how to skip stones
across the surface of the water.

And while Will's busy practicing,
Connor reaches out to give me the hug
I've been yearning for all morning . . .

But
just before
we actually touch each other,

Will somehow manages
to slip and fall
into the water.

And Connor and I have to race over
and yank the soggy little imp out,
before he giggles himself to death.

If I Didn't Know My Brother Better

I'd say he slipped into the creek
on purpose.

Oh, wait—
I *do* know him better.

And I'm pretty sure
he *did* do it on purpose.

But I guess
I can't blame the kid.

He's not trying
to keep Connor and me apart.

He's just trying
to get Connor's attention.

Which is probably because, like me,
Will's never even met his own dad.

So he's always looking
for father figures.

Mom swears she went to the sperm bank
to conceive both of us.

But I'm pretty sure she just says that
because she sleeps with so many guys

that she doesn't have a clue
who our *real* fathers are.

Mom Switches Boyfriends

More often than most people
switch lanes on the freeway.

It's like she's got
boyfriend ADD or something.

And her men don't exactly
make good father substitutes anyhow.

I mean,
all of them are actors.

So you'd think they'd be able to at least *act*
like they're interested in Will and me.

But except for the sicko
who tried to kiss me once,

none of Mom's lovers have made even
the slightest effort to get to know us.

It's Lunchtime

But Will's damp and chilled
from his dip in the creek.

So when we arrive
at Frank's Famous Hotdogs,

before we even sit down,
Connor heads directly to the cashier

and buys a T-shirt for him
to change into.

It's emblazoned with the words:
"Big Weenies Are Better."

Will slips it on,
then looks up at Connor and says,

"Thith ith, without a doubt,
the betht shirt I have ever owned."

"Looks great on you," Connor says,
bumping fists with him.

"And today'th been, without a doubt,
one of the betht dayth I have ever had."

"Me too," Connor says.
But he's looking right at *me*

when he says it.

Then—Inspiration Strikes

I send Will to ask the waitress
(who's clearing a table
at the far end of the restaurant)
if she can please come over and seat us.

The minute Will scampers off,
Connor and I exchange a glance,
rush to the nearest booth,
and slide into it.

He slips his arm around my shoulder,
presses his leg against mine,
and gives my knee a squeeze
with his free hand.

When I recover enough to speak,
I grin at him and say,
"I guess this proves that sometimes,
even where there's a *Will*,

there's a way."

A Second Later

When Will returns
and sees us sitting here,
he folds his arms across his chest.

"Hey . . . ," he says,
eyeing me suspiciously,
"I thought the *waitreth* had to theat uth."

"Oh . . . ," I say.
"Another waitress came by
and seated us while you were gone."

Connor gives me
a subtle little elbow nudge.
I give him one back.

And somehow,
being in cahoots with him
like this

feels so . . .
I don't know . . .
so intimate, I guess,

that my heart
starts beating faster
than the speed of light.

Is It My Imagination

Or is Connor's heart
beating faster too?

I swear I can feel it
fluttering against me

where our sides
are pressed together . . .

He gives my knee
another secret squeeze under the table.

Then he pats
the empty seat on his other side

and says to Will,
"I saved you a spot."

Will shoots Connor an adoring grin,
and scoots in next to him.

And when the waitress shows up
to take our order,

Will pounds the table
like a guy ordering drinks in a bar

and shouts,
"Bacon dogth for everybody!"

It Turns Out

That the weenies at Frank's
are even bigger than the weenie
on Will's new T-shirt.

But Will scarfs down a couple of them.
Plus a basket of fries
that's bigger than his head.

"You sure are packing it away," Connor says.
"Don't you think you ought
to take it easy?"

Will shrugs.
"I'm having another growth thpurt," he says.
"They make me mega hungry."

Then,
after a few more bites,
he says he has to go to the bathroom.

There happens to be one right across the aisle.
And it's the one-person kind.
So I let him go in alone.

A second later, the waitress stops by
to ask us if we want to order dessert.
Connor says, "I think I could go for a—"

But I give him a little kick under the table.
"Why don't you tell the waitress
why we're here?" I say.

Connor looks confused.
"Uh . . . for lunch?"
"You are such a riot," I say, rolling my eyes.

"I meant why don't you tell her about
the *celebration* we're having today?
You know—the one for *my brother?*"

"Ohhhhh . . . *that* celebration," he says.
"The one we're havin' because . . . uh . . .
because today is her brother's . . . um . . ."

The waitress
taps her pencil on her order pad.
"Because it's his . . . his . . ."

Geez.
I can't take it anymore.
"It's his *birthday*," I tell her.

"Oh!" she says with a smile.
"Why didn't you say so?
I'll be right back with some cake."

Then She Hurries Off

As soon as
she's out of earshot,
I give Connor a playful shove, and say,
"You couldn't lie your way out of a paper bag."

"Most girls," he replies,
flashing me a devastating smile,
"would consider that a *good* quality
in a boyfriend."

Omi*god.*
Did he just
refer to himself
as my *boyfriend*?

A Milky Way of stars
shoots all through me.
Connor searches my eyes,
then leans in to kiss me.

But
just before our lips meet,
we hear the sound of someone barfing.
And it's coming from the bathroom!

I Race Over and Knock on the Door

It inches open,
and I'll spare you
the gory details,

but a few
thoroughly disgusting
trying-not-to-gag minutes later,

I lead a pale,
slightly shaky Will
back over to our booth.

He glances at the table
and notices the big slice of fudge cake
that the waitress brought for him.

"Awwww," he says,
with a feeble grin.
"You remembered my birthday!"

But When Connor Offers the Cake to Him

Will says, "I don't think it would be
a good idea for me to eat that right now."
So Connor and I start feeding it
to each other, one forkful at a time.

Will watches us,
wrinkling up his nose.
"You're gonna make me barf
all over again."

When we finish the cake,
and the waitress brings the check,
I try to grab it.
But Connor beats me to it.

"Hey," I say. "Let *me* pay for lunch.
You've been paying for everything all day."
"It's no problem," Connor says. "Honest."
"Why?" Will asks. "Are you rich?"

Connor cracks up at this.
"My grandpa died and left me some money.
So I guess I *am* sort of rich."
Will brightens. "Jutht like *uth*!"

I give my brother
a will-you-*please*-shut-up look.
"He means *our* grandpa died, too," I explain.
"Not that we're rich."

"I'm sorry about your grandpa," Connor says.

"And I'm sorry about yours," I say.

"I'm thorry too!" Will says.

"You *ought* to be," I mutter under my breath.

Connor Tosses Some Bills
Onto the Table

Then
he grabs Will,
hoists him up for a piggyback ride,
and trots toward the door.

Will bounces along on Connor's back,
examining his hair at close range.
"Your hair makth you look jutht like a tiger.
Only without the pawth and the tail."

"Exactly the look I was going for," says Connor.
"Do you like animals, Will?"
"Nah," Will says. "I don't like 'em.
I *love* 'em!"

Connor laughs,
then roars and snarls,
pretending to sink his fangs into Will's arm.
Will giggles and pulls away.

"If you love animals," Connor says,
"I know just where to take you next."
Connor lowers Will to the ground and says,
"Come on. I'll tiger-race you to the car."

And
the two of them take off,
prowling and growling their way
through the parking lot.

Is it totally sick of me
to be feeling jealous
of my little brother
right now?

Don't answer that.

A Half Hour Later

When Connor's Cadillac
pulls up in front
of the Charles Paddock Zoo,
Will practically faints from joy.

He makes a beeline for the tigers.
"Look!" he says,
pointing Connor out to them.
"It'th your long lotht brother."

Then Will grabs hold of his hand
and never lets go of it—dragging him
from the pythons to the spider monkeys
to the gila monsters . . .

Until, finally, around an hour later,
Will gets so into looking at a four-eyed turtle
that he forgets himself,
and drops Connor's hand.

We exchange
a wavelengthy glance,
then tiptoe over to sit together
on the nearest bench.

Connor slips his arm around me
and I rest my head against his shoulder.
"I'm sorry about my brother," I say.
"He's been sticking to you like Velcro."

"That's okay," he says. "Will's a cool kid."
"I know . . . ," I say. "He's probably just fixating
on you because . . . well, because he's always
sort of on the lookout for father substitutes."

"How come?"
"Oh . . . because our own father . . .
our own father died when Will was a baby."
"Geez. Sorry to hear that. How'd it happen?"

"To tell you the truth . . . we never found out.
He was . . . he was in the CIA . . .
I'm not really supposed to talk about it.
But he went away on a business trip

and a week later, these two guys in black suits
showed up and told us he was never coming back.
They wouldn't even tell us how he died.
Said it was too top secret."

"That must've been awful," Connor says,
pulling me in for a hug.
"It *was* awful," I say,
melting into his arms.

And suddenly,
I'm blinking back tears.
Because sometimes
my lies are so good

I actually start believing them myself.

On the Drive Back to the Nirvana Inn

Will's so tired out,
that as soon as we hit the highway

he falls asleep and starts snoring
louder than a jackhammer.

Which makes it impossible for Connor
and me to carry on a conversation.

But,
at every red light,

when he takes his hand off the wheel
and reaches for mine,

we let our fingers
do the talking for us . . .

His Touch

So soft
and smooth,

swirling
across my wrist . . .

His thumb
tracing circles on my palm . . .

The pressure . . .
so achingly light . . .

I close my eyes,
and imagine

it's his tongue . . .

By the Time We Get Back to the Hotel

And the Caddy begins
its long, slow cruise
up the winding driveway,

all I can
think about
is kissing Connor.

I mean,
Will's earsplitting snoring
isn't exactly conducive to romance.

But I don't care anymore.
I can't go on like this.
Not for one more minute.

The instant the car stops,
I'm gonna grab Connor
and I'm gonna

kiss him.

We Roll Up to the Curb

He switches off the motor.
And I'm just about to pounce—

when Will pokes his head
into the front seat.

"How'd we get home tho fatht?" he asks,
rubbing his eyes.

Connor smiles his most tigery smile at me.
"We levitated," he says.

Will groans.
"We levitated and I *mitht* it?"

"We'll do it again," Connor says.
"Lots of times . . ."

And he's gazing so deeply
into my eyes when he says this

that I feel like he might
actually be seeing my soul.

Which is sort of scary.
But sort of wonderful, too . . .

"Well," I say. "I guess we better be going . . ."
"When can I see you again?" Connor says.

"Tell him he can thee uth tomorrow!" Will cries.
And Connor and I crack up.

"Why don't you text me later on?" I say.
"Why don't I text you right now?" he says.

He whips out his phone,
and punches in a message.

A second later my phone vibrates.
I open his text and read:

Tomorrow. You. Me.
Beach. Picnic. Alone.

It's Long After Midnight

But I can't fall asleep.
Because I can't stop thinking about Connor . . .

We haven't shared
a single kiss.

Not even the kind where you pretend
to aim for the other person's cheek

but then you let your lips drift over
onto the corner of their mouth

and linger for a split second longer
than they should . . .

He has never kissed me.
Not even once.

But I've kissed *him*—
again and again and again.

I've kissed him on beaches and in bathtubs
and in red leather booths,

kissed him on trains
and on planes

and in the deep shadows
of his Caddy's backseat.

I've kissed him
in elevators stuck between floors.

I've kissed him in cabins
by lonely lakes.

I've kissed him at the breathless tops
of neoned Ferris wheels.

I have kissed him
all over . . .

Suddenly

There's a light tap on my door.
I prick up my ears.

Maybe I imagined it . . .
I *must* have imagined it . . .

But now—
there's another tap!

The golden cupids snap to attention
and raise their bows.

I leap off the bed and rush over
to look through the peephole.

It's him!
Looking so hot it isn't even funny . . .

He's standing
right there,

and I'm standing here,
wearing nothing but a T-shirt and panties,

with just the thinnest slice of door
between us . . .

I reach for the knob,
yank it open, grab hold of his hand,

tug him into my room,
lead him up the stairs to the tower,

wrap my fingers
around the back of his neck,

and press my lips to his . . .
my hips to his . . .

And then . . .
then . . .

my mother shakes me awake.

Okay

So the truth is,
she *didn't* shake me awake.

Because
I wasn't dreaming.

I was just doing what I'm good at—
reinventing reality

and spinning it off
in a whole new direction.

Though,
you've got to admit,

that would've been
a ridiculously awesome dream.

And even *more* awesome
if it had actually happened . . .

On Saturday Morning

I'm getting dressed
for my beach picnic with Connor,

when Mom sweeps into my room
and says I better change out of my bikini

because she's taking Wilson and me
to the circus.

I say I have other plans.
She says what plans?

I say I met someone
and I'm spending the day with *him*.

But she says
she met someone, too.

I say let me guess—
his name's Jack, right?

Her eyebrows shoot up.
"How did you know?" she says.

I roll my eyes and say
well maybe it's because

you *always* have a thing with your costar
on every single movie you're in.

She looks a little wounded,
but shrugs off my snarky remark

and says she's afraid I'm going to
have to cancel my plans for today

because we're going to the circus with Jack
so that Wilson and I can get to know him.

I say why bother
getting to know him

when she's only going to dump him
as soon as the filming's over,

just like she dumps
all her *other* costars?

She says this one's different.
I say she says that *every* time.

She says well this time
it *is* different.

She says this time
she might be in love.

I say she says *that*
every time, too.

And,
for a minute,

she doesn't say
anything.

Then She Says

"You are *coming*
to the circus with us."

I say,
"No I'm not."

She says "'No I'm not'
is not an option."

I say, "What are you gonna do—
handcuff me and drag me to the circus?"

She ponders this for a while.
Then she says,

"If you come to the circus
with us today,

you can have dinner
with your new friend tonight."

I say, "Do you swear?"
And she says, "I swear to God."

So I say,
"Then you've got yourself a deal."

Which Is Why

Instead of spending the afternoon
with the guy I'm obsessed with,
I'm sitting here at a sucky circus,

with my brother
and my mother
and the guy *she's* obsessed with,

watching
the two of them
making googly eyes at each other

while
a tiger leaps
through flaming hoops

and my thoughts drift to tonight,
to the moonlit picnic on the beach
that I'll be sharing

with a certain *other* tiger.

So After the Circus

When Mom informs us
that Jack's taking us all out to dinner,
I nearly go ballistic.

I pull her aside and hiss, "We had a deal.
You swore if I went to the circus with you,
I could have dinner with *Connor*."

"Colette, darling," she coos.
"You *can* have dinner with Connor.
Just invite him to come along *with* us."

I'm so pissed at her,
steam's practically blasting
out of my ears.

I can't
believe I fell
for her lousy trick.

But I'd rather
walk over a bed of hot coals
than invite Connor to dinner with Mom.

Because if he meets her,
he'll find out I lied to him
about who she really is.

And besides,
the instant he lays eyes on her
he'll forget all about me,

and start panting and drooling
and asking her for her autograph.
Just like everyone *always* does.

So I decide to opt
for the bed of hot coals
instead.

And That's How Come

I had to text Connor
and tell him I was suffering
from food poisoning.

Obviously,
I was lying about
the food poisoning.

But that part
about the "suffering"
was a hundred percent true—

because instead of sitting on the beach
in the moonlight on a blanket
eating pizza with Connor right now,

listening
to the waves tell their secrets
to the shore,

I'm sitting here on a chair
made from recycled water bottles
eating hempseed-crusted tofu with Jack,

listening
to my mother
laugh at all his dumb jokes.

Even Will seems to think
Mom's new boyfriend
is hilarious.

And so do dozens of starstruck diners—
who are giggling and staring at our table
as if they're watching a movie.

It's Nine Thirty p.m.
and I'm Lying on My Bed

Imagining
that Connor's lying here
with me . . .

When suddenly,
there's a light tap on my door,
just like in that dream I had once.

Or did that happen
in one of the lies I told you?
Sometimes it's hard to keep track . . .

I rush over to peek through the peephole
and—it's him!
For *real*!

He's standing there
holding a bottle of Tums
with a fancy pink bow wrapped around it.

What a funny,
thoughtful,
incredible guy . . .

I grab hold of the knob,
and I'm just about to swing open the door
and fling myself into his arms,

when I glance at myself in the mirror
and realize that I do *not* look like someone
who's suffering from food poisoning.

I'm not
even slightly green
around the gills.

If I let Connor in,
he'll take one look at me
and know that I lied to him.

This calls for drastic measures!

I Race Toward the Bathroom

Shouting back
over my shoulder,
"I'll be right there!"

I grab some Goth Girl powder,
and brush it onto my face
to make my skin look pale.

I smudge some mascara onto my fingers
and rub it under my eyes
to make myself look tired.

But I'm so jittery,
I knock my hairbrush into the toilet,
splashing water all over my jeans.

I stifle a scream,
scramble out of them,
run to my closet,

yank on a clean pair,
sprint back over to the door,
and swing it open.

But—Connor's gone.

Damn It!

He must not have heard me
shout that I'd be right there.

Then I notice a note,
tucked under the bottle of Tums:

Colette,

I knocked, but you didn't answer.
Guess you were sleeping it off
or something.

Missed you today.
But absence is definitely making
my heart grow fonder.
Not to mention all my other
body parts.

Tomorrow's the Fourth of July.
You. Me. Beach. Picnic. Alone . . .

Fireworks!

I Flop Back Down on My Bed

And just lie here,
clutching his note
and the bottle of Tums
to my chest.

Then, all at once,
I get this overwhelming urge
to hear his voice—
so husky . . . so low . . . so . . . Connory . . .

I reach for my phone.
But at that very moment,
it starts ringing.
And it's him!

"I was just about to call *you*," I say.
"Yeah . . . I know," he says,
"It was like . . . like I could *feel* you
thinkin' of me."

My face goes all blotchy.
"Are you sure you aren't psychic?" I say.
"You know—
like that mentalist guy on TV?"

"I'm not psychic," he says.
"But you and me . . .
it's like we've got this . . .
this . . ."

"This *connection*," I say, finishing his sentence.
"Like when I woke up from my nap just now
and I got this real strong feeling
that I should open my door."

"So you found the Tums, huh?"
"Yes. Thanks! They're helping a lot.
And I'd *love* to spend the Fourth with you."
"And the fifth and the sixth too?" he says.

"Of course," I say.
Then, together, we say,
"And the seventh . . . and the eighth . . .
and the ninth . . ."

And then we share a dreamy silence.

How Times Change

If you'd have told me
a week and a half ago

that I'd be sleeping
with a bottle of Tums under my pillow,

I'd have told you
you were nuts.

But a lot can happen
in a week and a half.

And I really, really hope
that in the *next* week and a half

a whole lot *more*
will happen . . .

Though *Nothing* Is Going to Happen

If my mother keeps doing
everything in her power
to keep Connor and me apart.
In fact, here she comes now—

barging into my room
without even knocking
to tell me that Jack has
a "fantabulous Fourth of July" planned for us.

I hurl my pillow at the wall
and tell her that Connor and I
have a fantabulous Fourth
of our *own* planned.

But she says,
"I'm so sorry, darling.
I can't let you say no to Jack.
He'd be devastated.

Besides.
I'd love to meet
this Connor of yours.
Why don't you ask him to join us?"

And I'm so flustered
at the mere thought
of Connor meeting
my mother

that I blurt out the first lie
that darts into my head:
"He can't come with us.
He's working today."

"Oh?" she says with a smirk.
"I thought you two had plans . . .
But if he's working,
then I guess you're totally free

to spend the holiday with *us*."

I Hate It When That Happens

But I flat out refuse to give Mom
the satisfaction of admitting
she's caught me in another one of my lies.

Because if I do,
she'll start calling me Pinocchio.
And she won't stop for days.

She'll swear she can see
my nose growing.
She'll force me to call my shrink.

Though by then I'll *need*
to call my shrink because my mother
will have driven me stark raving mad

with all her stupid lectures
about how truth is beauty,
and beauty is truth

and blah . . .
blah . . . blah . . . blah . . .
blah . . . blah . . . blah . . .

That's why I can't even admit to
the puniest of lies—not even this tiny lie
about Connor having to work.

So I have no choice but to text him
and tell him that even though the Tums
are helping, I still feel sick.

Which is only
halfway untrue.
Because I *do* feel sick—

sick at the thought
of having to spend another whole day
away

from Connor.

The Worst July Fourth
in the History of July Fourths

First, Jack drags us up
to this teensy town called Cayucos
to see a sand castle contest.

Which might have seemed
sort of awesome
if I'd come with Connor.

Next,
Jack drags us over to watch
the Cayucos Independence Day parade—

with tons of über-hokey
floats and marching bands
and belly dancers,

and this whole gang of people,
all dressed in yellow, chanting:
"Eat! Bananas! Eat! Eat! Bananas!"

Which might have seemed
sort of hilarious
if I'd come with Connor.

After that, Jack drags us down
to the Veterans Hall to play bingo
with all these crusty old ladies.

Which might have seemed
sort of fun,
in an ironic kind of way,

if I'd come with Connor.

After Bingo

Jack drags us over
to an oyster bar for lunch,
and does an elaborate demonstration
for Will and me on the proper way
to eat the revolting things.

"You gotta swallow 'em whole," he says.
"While they're still alive and kicking."
He chooses an oyster from the platter,
brings it up to his lips,
and says,

"These little critters
were the original sliders."
I try not to gag as he tilts his head back
and lets it slither down his throat
without even chewing it.

Then he turns to Will
and says, "How about you, my man?
Are you brave enough to try one?"
Will turns whiter than the oysters,
but he smiles grimly

and says, "I thertainly am."
Jack hands an oyster to Will.
He raises it to his trembling lips,
squeezes his eyes closed,
and lets it slip down his throat.

He shudders
and almost coughs it right back up,
but somehow manages to keep it down.
Mom bursts into applause.
Will and Jack high-five each other.

"I *did* it!" Will cries.
"That wath mega cool!"
Then Jack says, "What about you, Colette?
You're not gonna let your baby brother
show you up, are you?"

This guy must be
even dumber than he looks,
if he thinks he's going to shame me
into swallowing a live animal that resembles
a glob of phlegm someone hacked up.

"Sorry," I say.
"I think I'll stick with fish and chips.
I make it a point
never to eat my lunch
until it's dead."

My mother nails me with a look,
but Jack just laughs,
and slips another
gleaming phlegm ball
down his throat,

while a group of middle-aged women,
who've been ogling him
from the table next to ours,
sucks in a collective breath,
like this is the most thrilling thing

they've ever seen in their lives.

All During the Rest of the Meal

Jack pretends
he's super interested
in getting to know Will and me,
asking us these epically lame questions—

like who our favorite rap stars are
and what our hobbies are
and which one of his movies
do we think he was the most amazing in?

Okay. So he didn't actually ask that last question.
But he sure is fishing for compliments.
He's practically down on his knees
begging for them.

Seriously.
You don't want to know
what agony
this lunch is.

And it gets even worse when Will and Jack
start trading knock-knock jokes.
Which is when I realize that my brother's
actually beginning to *like* this guy.

And, I mean, I feel for the kid, you know?
Every time he starts to bond with another one
of my mother's costar boyfriends,
the filming ends and so does her romance.

Leaving Will as fatherless as ever.
I learned long ago to keep my emotional
distance from Mom's boyfriends.
But Will's a hopeless optimist.

The poor little sucker.

After Lunch

Jack drives us back to the hotel,
where we settle into Mom's room
for a rollicking game of Chutes and Ladders.

Followed by
a rollicking game
of Hungry Hungry Hideous Hippos.

If it weren't for the funny texts
Connor keeps sending me,
I think I might literally die of boredom . . .

Then, halfway through
a rollicking game of Candy Land,
Jack gets this weird look on his face.

He grabs his stomach,
and, without a word, he leaps up
and bolts into Mom's bathroom.

"Jack?" Mom calls after him, "Are you okay?"
But a second later, she grabs *her* stomach,
and hurries off to her other bathroom.

Will and I exchange a glance and a giggle.
"Mutht have been the oythterth," Will says.
"I'm lucky I only ate one of—"

But he stops in mid-sentence,
clutches his belly and turns chalk white.
"Uh oh . . . ," he says.

Then, he races across the room,
yanks open the connecting door,
and vrooms into *his* bathroom.

I pause briefly to reflect
on the irony that I am the only one
without food poisoning,

before calling down to Dexter,
asking him to send up a doctor,
and rushing next door to help Will.

Fifteen Minutes Later

The producer and the director
of *Love Canoe*
are pacing around Mom's room
talking in hushed tones,

while a doctor
examines the patients,
and Dexter delivers trays of tea and toast,
his Adam's apple oddly still.

An hour after that,
when the three patients
are finally asleep,
a night nurse arrives to look after them.

I tiptoe over to Will's bedside,
plant a kiss
on his clammy little forehead,
then slip away

to meet Connor!

I Fly Through the Lobby
and Out the Front Door

There he is!
Leaning against a wall
next to his motorcycle,

looking
even hotter
than I remember him looking—

his hands jammed deep
into the pockets
of his leather jacket,

his ankles crossed,
his black round-toed boots
scuffed to perfection,

his amber eyes
reflecting the glow
of the light from the lamppost,

and
that hair . . .
that *hair* of his!

When He Catches Sight of Me

He flashes me
a knee-wobbling smile

and gives me
that funny little salute of his.

He takes a quick step
in my direction.

But then he stops,
and lets me come to *him*.

I slow my pace and stroll over,
till we're just a couple of feet apart.

And then, at the exact same instant,
we say, "Long time no see."

Stunned,
we both say, "Whoa . . ."

And then we laugh
and reach to hug each other.

But, just before we touch—
pop!pop!pop!pop!pop!

Some kids playing with firecrackers
interrupt us.

Connor says, "We better go.
Don't wanna miss the fireworks."

We climb onto his motorcycle,
I wrap my body around his,

and we blaze off into the sunset
like a flaming meteor.

Twenty Minutes Later

We arrive in Pismo Beach
and run through the crowd
toward the pier.

The moment
we reach the water's edge,
the fireworks begin—

as if
the people
in charge of setting them off

have been waiting
for Connor and me
to arrive.

And just
as the first rockets
whiz into the sky,

and their neon umbrellas
burst open
over our heads,

Connor
pulls me to him
and presses his lips

to mine.

Softly at First . . .

Then his kiss
spreads all through me
like a fever.

And a strange breathless
heart-pounding feeling
washes over me—

this feeling like
I've finally found
the rest of me,

the part of me that,
until just a minute ago,
I didn't even know existed.

I've Kissed Other Boys

But
before tonight

I never knew
that I could *ignite*.

I can't believe
what I've been missing—

this
kissing . . .

this
blissing . . .

this
*this*sing!

It's After Midnight

And I'm soaking
in a tub full of bubbles,

watching wisps of steam
rise and swirl and curl,

the candlelight bathing everything
in a rosy shimmering glow

as I relive
my date with Connor . . .

I'm not quite sure whether
kissing him for the very first time

while the fireworks
were literally exploding overhead

was the corniest moment
in the history of kissing

or the most romantic moment
ever experienced

between two people
on the face of the earth.

On Monday Morning

The doctor says
Mom and Jack can go back to work,
but that Will should lay low.
So I invite Connor over to hang out with us.

He shows up
with a deck of cards,
and proceeds to do
a mind-blowing trick for us—

where he has me write my name on a card,
and slip it back into the middle of the deck.
And then, a few seconds later,
it turns up in Will's pocket!

"Oh no you didn't . . . ," I say.
"Oh yeth he *did*!" Will cries.
"Want me to teach you how?" Connor asks Will.
"Duth a bear poop in the woodth?" he replies.

And while Will's busy
practicing the trick,
Connor and I sneak off into my room
and start making out on the couch.

But suddenly,
Will's standing right next to us,
saying, "Ewww. Get a room, you two."
"I wish we *could*," Connor mutters.

And that's when I get a brilliant idea.

I Ask Will If He Wants
to Play Hide-and-Seek

Because I know from experience
exactly what he'll say:
"I thertainly do! And *I* want to be 'it'!"

"Well . . . okay," I say. "But you have to count
to three hundred—to give Connor and me
time to find truly excellent hiding places."

Then I suggest
that to make it even more fun,
we can either hide in Will's room or in mine.

"Thweeeet . . . ," Will says.
We lead him back into his room,
and settle him in on his couch.

He shuts his eyes
and begins counting:
"One . . . two . . . three . . ."

"No peeking," I say,
as I grab Connor's hand
and tug him into my room.

I put a finger to my lips,
then point to the winding staircase
that leads to the tower.

We tiptoe up the steps.
And when we reach the top,
Connor whispers, "Beautiful view up here . . ."

But he's not
looking out the window.
He's looking at *me*.

We'll only be alone till Will finds us.
But we sure will make the most of it
till then . . .

"153 ... 154 ... 155 ..."

I lose myself in Connor's lips . . .
in the heat of his hands . . .
in the press of his hips . . .

Then, all of a sudden,
I realize that Will
has stopped counting.

And a second later,
I become aware
of a voice.

My mother's voice!
And it's coming
from Will's room!

"Wilson darling," she's saying,
"where's Colette?
Why are you in here all alone?"

"Oh, I'm not alone," he says.
"We're playing hide-and-theek.
And I'm 'it.'"

Then he goes right back
to counting:
"281 . . . 282 . . . 283 . . ."

But then
I hear Mom's stilettos
clicking toward *my* room.

It's too late to smuggle Connor out!
"My mother will kill me
if she finds you here," I whisper.

Which isn't even slightly true.
But *I'll* kill *myself*
if Connor finds out

who my mother really is.

Connor Pretends to Zip His Lips

I give him one last fierce kiss,
then zoom down the stairs and fling myself
onto my bed just as Will says, "298 . . . 299 . . .
300! Ready or not, here I come!"

He barrels into my room and his face falls.
"Hey," he says. "Why aren't you hiding?"
"Let's finish the game later," I say,
"so that Mom can tell us about her day."

"She can tell *you* about her day," he says,
"I wanna look for—"
"For that *deck of cards* you lost?" I interrupt,
shooting him a please-don't-give-me-away look.

He narrows his eyes at me, but goes along with it.
"Yeah," he says, "And when I find them,
I'll do a card trick for Mom.
The one that *Connor* taught me."

"I didn't know he was a magician," Mom says.
"He ith," Will says.
"Which ith why he'th perfect for Colette—
they *both* know a lot of *trickth* . . ."

"Anyone hungry?" I say,
trying to change the subject.
"Starved," Mom says,
flopping down next to me on the bed.

"But I'm too tired to go out.
Let's have room service."
"Order me a burger," Will says. "And I'll keep
looking for that thneaky little . . . *deck of cardth*."

He streaks over to the closet and whips it open.
"Not in here . . . ," he says.
He gets down on his belly
to look under the bed.

He peeks behind the couch
and all the drapes.
Then he scoots into the bathroom
and yanks apart the shower curtains.

Mom chuckles and calls out,
"Do you think the cards wanted a bath?"
"You never know . . . ," Will says,
as he sprints out of the bathroom.

He pauses to scan the room,
then his face brightens,
and before I can stop him
he scampers right past me,

and dashes up the winding staircase.

I Hold My Breath

Will gasps.
Then he cries, "Gotcha!"

My heart crashes to my feet
like a lead brick.

A second from now,
Connor will walk down those stairs,

find out that my mother
is Marissa Shawn,

and fall so completely
under her spell

that he'll forget
I even—

"Look what *I* found!" Will yells.
And he comes clomping down the steps

waving Connor's
deck of cards.

I Run Over to My Brother

And give him a bear hug.
"Great job of . . . finding those cards!" I say.
He wiggles out of my arms,
beaming brighter than a lighthouse.

Then he trots over to Mom,
who's still sprawled across my bed.
"Come to *my* room now," he says to her,
"I wanna show you the trick."

"Can't you just show it to me right here?"
He sneaks me a conspiratorial wink and says,
"No. There'th a . . . a better table in there.
It'th my . . . my *lucky* table."

Then he grabs hold
of both her hands,
tugs her up,
and drags her out of the room.

Boy . . .
I owe that kid
a truckload
of gummy worms!

I Follow Them Into Will's Room

And remind Mom
that we still haven't ordered dinner.

I offer to call room service
while Will dazzles her with his card trick.

"I know Will wants a burger," I say,
"but what do *you* want?"

I take her order,
then stroll nonchalantly into my room,

closing, and quietly locking,
the door behind me.

Then I bound
up the winding staircase.

But when I reach the top—
Connor's gone.

He must have snuck out
when I was in the other room.

And the only sign
that he was even there

is the king of hearts lying on the floor,
with a single word scrawled across it:

Tomorrow?

Tuesday Morning

It's only nine a.m.,
but it's already eighty degrees outside
and Will's nagging me to bring him to the pool.

So as soon as Mom heads to the set,
I text Connor: **Put on ur snorkel mask
and get over here.**

Ten minutes later,
there's a knock at my door.
I look through the peephole—and it's him!

I whip open the door, and Will rushes up
to throw his arms around him,
beating me to it.

"How'd you get here so fast?" I say.
He blushes, in that devastating way of his,
and says, "I live pretty close by."

When we arrive at the pool,
it's still so early in the morning
that no one else is here yet.

Connor slips off
his T-shirt and jeans,
while I try to act like it's no big deal.

But when I see
the delicate arrow
of golden hairs

leading down
into his swim trunks,
my cheeks go all blotchy.

And when I take off my robe
and feel Connor's eyes traveling
over every inch of me,

my
whole *body*
goes all blotchy.

Then

The three of us ease into
the mirror-smooth warm water,
and, right away, Connor says,
"Let's play Marco Polo."

The instant Will closes his eyes
and shouts, "Marco!"
Connor grabs me and kisses me.
"Marco!" Will shouts again.

Connor tears his lips from mine
just long enough to shout back, "Polo!"
Then he covers my lips
with his again.

"Marco!" Will calls.
I yank my mouth from Connor's
and shout back, "Polo!"
Then I lean in for more kisses.

"Marco!"
Kisskisskisss.
"Polo!"
Kisskisskiss.

"Marco!"
Kisskisskisss.
"Polo!"
Kisskisskiss.

God . . .
I could play
this game
all day . . .

But It's Not Long Before
Will Sneaks a Peek

And catches us making out.
He shakes his finger at us
and says, "Have you no shame?"

Then he starts shrieking with laughter
and splashing us and leaping all over us,
trying to pry us apart.

There's a flash of murder in Connor's eyes.
He shoves Will away and starts
splashing him back with a vengeance.

Connor's acting
like it's all in good fun,
but I can tell he's pissed off.

My mouth goes dry as sand.
How much more of this
will he be able to put up with

before he stops coming around?

When Connor Goes Home

I sit Will down
and try to explain to him
why he *has* to stop
bugging Connor and me.

And, I mean,
he's a good kid,
and he wants me to be happy,
but self-control is not his strong suit.

And besides—
he's just
too young
to get it.

Which is why,
after suffering through a couple more
jaw-clenchingly excruciating days
as a threesome,

I decide
that the time has come
to resort
to drastic measures.

So

On Friday morning,
I get up ridiculously early,
slink down to the lobby,

and grab
a wedge of lemon
from the Cloud Nine Café.

Then I bolt back up to my room
and squeeze a couple of drops of juice
into each of my eyes.

It stings something awful,
but achieves the desired effect—
I look like I've been crying my eyes out.

Next, I smudge
a little bit of mascara under my eyes
to make it look like I haven't slept a wink.

And now,
I'm ready to slip out into the hall,
tiptoe past Will's room,

and knock on Mom's door.

When It Swings Open

She takes one look at me,
and sweeps me into a theatrical hug.
"Colette, darling. What's the matter?"

This is my cue.
I tell her that Connor and I
almost broke up last night.

I tell her that he said he really likes me,
but he just doesn't think he can handle
dating me *and* my little brother anymore.

I tell her I've never felt this way
about anyone before—
that I think I might be falling in love.

And this last part,
at least,
is true.

Mom's Eyes Tear Up

"First love . . . ," she murmurs,
wistfully brushing my bangs off my forehead.
"First love is . . . well, it's a beautiful thing."

"Yeah," I say, in my most pitiful voice.
"But not if the two of you
can never *ever* be alone together."

"I'm so sorry, sweetheart," she says.
"I had no idea babysitting for Wilson
was putting such a cramp in your style."

"Oh, that's okay," I say.
"You've been so busy with work . . .
And with getting to know Jack . . ."

Mom looks down at her feet.
Her cheeks flush with what I hope
is an attack of crushing guilt.

Then she looks back up at me
and says, "If you can just hang
on till tomorrow morning,

Jack and I will take your brother up to Big Sur
for the weekend, so you and Connor can have
a couple of days to patch things up."

Whoa . . .
Thank you, lemon juice!
Thank you, mascara!

Thank you, ye benevolent gods of romance!

The Rest of the Day

Flits by in a blur
of babysitting
and breathless anticipation . . .

Connor and I
drive Will up to San Simeon
to show him the elephant seals.

We take him
to lunch at Sebastian's
and celebrate his "birthday."

We take him to the Hearst Castle
to see if he can spot
any wild zebras.

And for the first time ever,
we don't try to steal any kisses.
Or even to hold hands.

Because the whole Will-less weekend
lies stretched out before us
like a path leading straight

to heaven.

It's Almost One in the Morning.

And I'm trying to fall asleep.
But I feel like I just drank
a dozen cans of Red Bull.

And I can't stop wondering
what will be happening tomorrow night
right here in this bed . . .

I have no idea
whether or not I'm ready
to go all the way with Connor.

But something tells me
I'll have a chance
to find out.

He's eighteen—
so I'm sure he's not a virgin.
And he probably thinks *I'm* not either.

Because I told him I was eighteen too.
Which seemed like a good idea
at the time.

But what would he think if he knew
that I've never been to third base?
And that I haven't even—*bzzzttt!*

It's a text.
From Connor!
Thinking about me?

I Text Him Right Back

**Yes.
I AM thinking
about u.**

Good,
he texts back.
Becuz guess what?

**I'm standing right outside ur door.
Wanna get this party started
a little early?**

Whoops . . .

There I go again—
reinventing reality.

I mean, Connor did send me a text
to ask me if I was thinking about him.

But, alas, he wasn't standing
right outside my door when he sent it.

And speaking of Connor,
sometimes I wonder

how he'd feel if he knew
what a liar I was.

He's the most
honest person I've ever met.

He couldn't even handle
telling the waitress it was Will's birthday.

If he knew about my . . . my little addiction,
how would he react?

I sure hope I never
get the chance to find out . . .

On Saturday Morning

I help Will cram his footie pajamas,
his stuffed raccoon, his bathing suit,
and the fart machine that Connor gave him
into his backpack.

"I wish you were coming with uth," Will says.
"We're gonna go whale watching
and rent a boat and go fishing and thnorkling
and it'th gonna be mega cool!"

"It certainly is," says Jack,
as he strides through the door,
hoists Will up over his shoulder with one hand,
and grabs his backpack with the other.

"What's *in* here?" Jack says. "An anvil?"
"You'll find out . . . ," Will says mysteriously.
Then Jack turns to me and says, "Sure you won't
change your mind and come with us?"

"I wish I could," I say. "But—"
"She needth to have alone time with Connor for
kithing and all that other yucky thtuff teenth do."
I can feel my cheeks going all blotchy.

"Who told you *that*?" I say.
"Mom did," he says.
"It figures," Jack says, and we both crack up.
"That mother of yours is a true original, Cola."

Cola? Gimme a break.
Since when did Jack assign me a nickname?
And why is he acting like we're old buddies?
He doesn't even *know* me.

"You and your brother are true originals too.
But Wonka here's starting to break my back.
We better head down to the car.
Why don't you come see us off?"

Wonka . . . ?

We Head Down
to the Front of the Hotel

Where Mom's trying to finish stuffing
their things into the trunk of Jack's Porsche,
while fending off a mob of autograph hounds.

When they see Jack coming,
they abandon Mom
and hurry over to accost *him*.

She looks both relieved and hurt,
but takes this opportunity
to pop a silver box into my hands.

"A present?" I say. "For me?"
"For you," she says, getting weirdly misty-eyed.
"Because . . . because you're in love."

I begin to untie the pink satin ribbon,
but she covers my hands with hers
to stop me.

"Why don't you wait to open it
until after we leave?" she says.
"Okay, Mom. Thanks."

She gazes into my face for a second.
"Have a fabulous weekend," she says.
"But . . . well . . . just be careful, okay?"

"Don't worry, Mom. We're only
planning on smoking a *little* crack."
She laughs, and gives me a quick squeeze.

Then they all hop into the car.
And as it pulls away,
and the disappointed mob drifts off,

Will sticks his head
out the window and hollers back to me,
"Happy thmooching!"

I roll my eyes and wave good-bye,
then untie the ribbon,
and ease the lid off the box.

There,
nesting in a cloud
of pink tissue paper—

are a zillion condoms!

No, Really

There *are*.
I swear I'm not making this up!

And I don't know
which is more embarrassing—

the fact that my mother
just gave me condoms,

or the fact that she gave me
so *many*.

She must have done it
because I told her I was in love . . .

Most moms do everything they can
to keep their daughters from having sex.

My mom's always told me
that if I was in love,

I should just go for it.

The Problem Is

I have no idea if I *am* in love.
Or if I'm ready to "go for it" or not.

And I'm so freaked out
by the sight of the condoms,

blinking up at me
in their little tinfoil packages,

that I slam the lid
back down on the box.

But my fingers slip,
the box goes flying,

and the condoms skitter off
in all directions

like a handful
of insanely shiny mice . . .

I Drop Down Onto My Knees

Scrambling
to pick them all up,

and start jamming them
back into the box.

There is a very real possibility
that I'm gonna have a heart attack right now . . .

I mean,
there are people all around me.

And a couple of them
are snickering and snapping photos!

Suddenly, I become aware
of a thundering roar.

Is it the sound
of my heart pounding?

But when
I glance up—

I see
Connor's motorcycle

zooming
up the driveway!

I Freeze

And
for a split second,
I think I might actually faint.

Connor hasn't noticed me yet,
but he's pulling into the parking lot
only fifty feet away from me!

I shift into warp speed,
my fingers scuttling across the cement
like crazed crabs,

trying
to snatch up the rest
of the condoms.

But my hands are so shaky,
it's hard to get a grip
on the wafer-thin packages.

And
even harder
to get a grip on *myself*.

Because when I shoot a glance
in Connor's direction,
I see that he's walking toward me now—

and
he's already
halfway here!

He's Already Halfway Here!

And I'm squatting
like a freaking idiot

in the center
of a contraceptive crop circle,

my arms moving so fast now
they're actually blurring—

like I've turned into some kind
of cartoon octopus.

Then finally,
finally,

when Connor's only
fifteen feet away from me,

I manage to scrape
the last one off the sidewalk.

I stuff it into the box with the others,
bang down the lid,

spring to my feet,
and shove it behind my back.

But It's Too Late

Connor sees
that I'm hiding something.

"Whatcha got there?" he asks,
trying to get a better look.

I'm so flustered
it isn't even funny.

I can't even think up a good lie.
"It's . . . it's nothing," I say lamely.

"A box full of nothin'?" he says.
"Sounds intriguing . . ."

He reaches behind me playfully,
and tries to pry it from my hands.

But I yank it away from him, and shove it
deep into the recesses of my purse.

Then I grab him
and kiss him so hard

that he forgets
all about it.

The Next Thing I Know

We're lying on my bed,
drifting in each other's arms

under a hazy blanket
of golden sun.

I'm not even sure
how we got here—

I guess
we must have floated,

or dreamed
ourselves here,

or wished
a wish so strong

that we somehow made it
come true.

Then

There's nothing but his lips . . .
his tongue . . .

his hands
slipping under my tee . . .

his heart
a wild drum . . .

nothing but our bodies
saying, "Wow . . ."

nothing but Connor . . .
nothing but me . . .

and this heat . . .
this need . . .

this *now*.

All of a Sudden

His hands
are gliding back out
from under my shirt
and before I even grasp
what's happening,
he's taking hold
of its soft cotton fabric
and with one fluid motion
he's sliding it off over my head,
pressing his cheek
against the lacy cup of my bra,
his tiger stripes brushing
across my bare skin
for the very first time . . .

And it all
feels so great . . .
so incredibly great . . .

But
so
out
of control

and
I can't
catch my

breath . . .

And Now

He's reaching behind my back,
his fingers on a frenzied mission
to undo the hook of my bra.

And suddenly things start to feel
like they're moving too fast,
but in this strange slow-motiony sort of way.

And I realize that I want him to stop.
That I need him to stop.
Now.

"Wait . . . ," I say. *"Wait."*
But he doesn't
wait.

"Please . . . ," I say. "Stop."
But he doesn't
stop.

"Stop!" I say again,
wrapping my fingers around his wrists
to pull his hands away from the hook.

"For chrissake . . . ," Connor groans.
A storm gathers in his eyes.
"Sorry . . . ," I whisper. "I'm so sorry . . ."

Connor blinks and the storm's gone.
He gives his head a sharp shake,
and cradles my face with his hands.

"Don't be sorry . . . ," he says,
"*I'm* the one who should be sorry.
I shouldn't have pushed it.

We'll take it slow from now on.
We'll take it nice and slow.
As slow as you want."

Then he kisses me on my forehead
and adds, "We've got all day . . .
all night . . . all weekend long . . ."

And That's When I Notice

That the golden cupids
seem to be winking at me,

aiming their bows and arrows
directly at my purse,

where it lies on the nightstand,
nonchalant as a cat—

one gleaming corner of the silver box
full of you-know-whats

peeking
out,

shimmering
like there's no tomorrow . . .

A Little Shiver Zings Down My Spine

I sit up
and fold my arms over my chest,
feeling very shirtless all of a sudden.

Connor seems to understand.
He reaches for my tee
and helps me slip it back on.

Then he says, "I was in such a rush
to get over here and see you this mornin'
that I didn't have time for breakfast."

He glances at the clock.
"It's almost noon," he says. "You hungry?"
"Starved," I say.

Then we get on that wavelength of ours,
and, at the exact same moment,
we shout, "Room service!"

I dig the menu out of the nightstand drawer,
surreptitiously shoving the silver box
out of sight.

But *not* out of mind . . .

We Look Through the Menu

And decide on bacon burgers and fries,
with extra sides of bacon (of course).
"Want to order some milkshakes, too?" I say.

"I'd rather order champagne," he says.
"Can we even *do* that?" I say.
"Neither of us is twenty-one . . ."

"It's room service,"
he says with an impish grin.
"They'll think they're talkin' to your mother."

So I call in the order, trying my best to
sound like Mom, and just before I hang up,
I tell them it's Connor's birthday.

He grins and says, "How did you know?"
"Know what?"
"That today's my birthday."

"You're kidding, right?"
"Nope. I turned nineteen today.
You are officially dating an older man."

"Omigod," I say.
"You should have told me.
I would have given you a present."

"You still *can* give me a present," he says,
pulling me in for a soul-stirring hug.
"All I want for my birthday

is you."

All He Wants . . . Is Me?

My heart
shifts into overdrive.

And it's still thumping like mad
when the waiter arrives.

He wheels in a table
covered with gleaming silver domes,

a small vase of pink roses,
and a frosty bottle of champagne.

Then he discreetly scans the room,
as if he's looking for someone.

I figure I better leap in, before he asks
for "Ms. Shawn" in front of Connor.

"My mom's taking a shower," I tell him.
"But she said I could sign for it."

The waiter doesn't even bat an eyelash at this.
He just nods and hands me the check.

Connor gives me a subtle thumbs-up.
I flash him back a secret smile.

And while the waiter uncorks the champagne
and swivels it into a bucket of ice,

I forge my mother's illegible signature.
Then I hand the check back to the waiter.

He gives us a butlery bow
and quietly slips out the door.

The instant
it swings shut behind him,

Connor sprints over
to lock it.

When He Turns to Face Me

His eyes
are so bright
and his cheeks are so flushed

and he just looks so . . .
I don't know . . . so adoring, I guess . . .
and so adorable,

that I practically melt
into a puddle
right here on the floor.

"We need some mood lighting," he says,
dashing over to the curtains
to pull them closed.

And,
in the thrilling blink of an eye,
the room's as dark as midnight.

But a Second Later
I Hear a Loud *Thwack*

Followed by an even louder "Ouch!"
And I can't help cracking up.
"Maybe there's a little *too* much
mood lighting," I say.

"My big toe agrees with you," he says.
I feel my way along the wall to the bathroom
to get my orange-blossom candle, then I light it
and set it down next to the champagne.

"Brilliant . . . ," Connor says.
He rolls the table to the foot of the bed,
and we settle in beside it on the comforter,
sitting next to each other.

He reaches for the bottle
and pours the champagne.
It whispers faintly
as it fizzes into our glasses.

And for a while,
we just sit here together,
watching the bubbles float to the top
in endless dreamy streams . . .

Then I Clink My Glass Against His

And say, "To the birthday boy."
And he clinks his against mine
and says, "To the birthday boy's girlfriend."

We turn to face each other,
lock eyes,
and take our first frothy sip—

so foamy
and tingly and creamy
all at once,

like a tiny wave
breaking on the shore
of my tongue.

Then We Take Another Sip

And another
and another and another . . .

And soon we're giggling
like little kids

and feeding each other
strips of bacon

and washing them down
with more champagne and more,

till I can feel the bubbles
bubbling all through me like soapsuds

and we're rolling around on the comforter
and tickling each other and laughing

and the golden cupids
are laughing too

and the room's spinning
into a dizzy blur

and everything's glowing and floating
and we're kissing and laughing

and kissing
and groping

and kissing
and kissing and kissing . . .

And Now His Hand . . .

His hand's
gliding around behind me . . .
slipping under my tee . . .

stroking
the small of my back
with his long warm fingers . . .

his touch so light
my whole body's
vibrating . . .

And now he's kissing my neck,
murmuring, "We'll take things slow . . .
As slow as you want . . ."

And he's lifting
my T-shirt off
over my head,

one of his hands floating up
to cup the lace
of my bra,

his other hand
drifting down
onto my bare stomach,

his fingers
moving back and forth
across it . . .

Now lower . . . and lower . . .
till they're almost grazing
the top of my jeans . . .

And He's Whispering My Name

Whispering it
again and again,
as if it's a magic spell . . .

And a hunger's rising in me
like the endless streams of bubbles
rising in the champagne . . .

And suddenly
his fingers are fumbling
with the button on my jeans.

And he's whispering, "Colette . . .
Colette . . . Co*lette* me . . . let me . . .
let me . . ."

And Then

I feel the button on my jeans give way,
feel Connor's fingers unzipping them!
And then I hear *another* zipper!

My heart's beating so fast.
Faster than any heart has ever beaten before.
It's all too much . . . way too much . . .

And he's working his hand into my pants,
and I'm grabbing hold of his wrist
and pulling it back out again,

saying, "Hold on . . . Hold on a second . . ."
And he's murmuring, "What . . . ? Oh. Right . . .
Wanna use mine or one of yours?"

"One of my what?"
"One of your condoms.
You know—in that silver box of yours."

My heart comes to a dead halt.
"You *saw* them?" I say.
"You saw the condoms?"

"Yeah," he says with an innocent shrug.
"I peeked in the box when you
were signin' the check.

That's how I knew
we were on the same
wavelength."

Then he leans in and kisses me,
deep and drunk and sloppy,
and mumbles in my ear,

"Let's use 'em all tonight . . ."

My Stomach Clenches

And then I'm rolling away from him
and pushing up from the bed,
weaving a little on unsteady legs.

Connor looks
as shocked as if I'd just slapped him
across the face.

He flings himself
onto his back
and groans.

Or maybe it's more like a growl.
"You're killin' me, babe . . .
You're *killin'* me here."

His hands fly up to hold his head,
like he's trying to keep it
from exploding.

"I don't get it . . . ," he says.
"Why are you acting
like you're some kind of virgin?

I thought you *wanted* to . . .
I mean, why else would you have
all those condoms?"

I'm much too wasted
to lie my way out of this one.
So I just say, "It's . . . it's hard to explain."

Connor laughs a hollow laugh,
and says, "Yeah, I guess it is.
But, oh well . . .

Happy birthday to me, right?"

Oh, God . . .

I can't believe this.
I've totally ruined his birthday.

I sit back down on the edge of the bed
and try to hug him.

But he holds up a hand
to keep me away.

"All this 'stop,' 'go,' 'yes,' 'no'—
I can't take it."

"I know," I say helplessly.
"I'm sorry . . ."

"I want to show you how I feel," he says.
"I *need* to show you.

And it's so hard . . .
Too hard to hold back."

Then he heaves himself out of the bed,
gives me that funny little salute of his,

and lurches out the door.

For a Minute

I just sit here
on my suddenly empty bed,

watching the door ease shut
behind him.

Then I leap up,
stagger across the room,

swing it back open,
and bolt out into the hall,

calling, "Connor!
Connor, come back!"

But he's already
gone.

I Stand Here for a Second

In a drunken stupor,
the reality of what's happened
ripping into me like a dull blade.

Connor is gone . . .
He's gone . . .
Gone.

Then, I turn around
to drag myself back
toward my room—

just in time
to see the door
click shut.

I try
the knob,
but it's locked.

And that's when it dawns on me
that I don't have my room key.
Or my cell phone.

Or my shirt.

I Pound Uselessly on the Door

Then I sink down onto the floor in front of it,
hug my knees to my chest,
and start sobbing so hard it isn't even funny.

And just then,
the door of the room across the hall
begins to open!

I swallow a scream,
my eyes darting everywhere at once,
searching frantically for somewhere to hide.

Which is when I see
the remains of someone's lunch
sitting on a table a few doors down.

I streak over to it
and dive underneath
its floor-length tablecloth,

just as a family with three little kids
spills out into the hall
and heads in my direction.

I Hold My Breath

And wait for them to pass,
praying they won't notice
that the tablecloth's fluttering.

I follow their progress
through a tiny hole
in the fabric,

and heave
a silent sigh of relief
when they pass right by me.

But then the littlest kid,
who looks about three years old,
doubles back.

And a second later,
he lifts up a corner of the cloth,
bringing the two of us face to face.

Because
that's the kind of day
I'm having.

He Doesn't Even Seem Surprised to See Me

As if he's *always*
lifting up tablecloths and finding
shirtless girls crouched beneath them.

He stares at me,
unblinking, solemn.
Then he says, "Hi."

I hold my finger up to my lips
and shake my head in a silent plea
for him not to let on that I'm here.

He cocks his head to the side,
stares at me for a while,
then hollers down the hall to his family:

"Hey evwybody!
Come say hi to de unduhwear lady
who's hiding unduh de table."

Oh, geez . . .
I am doomed . . .
I am so totally freaking doomed . . .

But then I hear his family chuckling.
"Carter, honey," his mother calls,
"you've got such a great imagination."

"Come on, son!" his father shouts.
"Say good-bye to your new 'friend.'
The elevator's here."

Carter grins at me,
and says, "Bye-bye."
Then he scampers off to join his family.

And it isn't until a few moments later,
when I hear the sound
of the elevator doors whooshing closed,

that my heart slows down,
till it's only beating twice as fast
as normal.

I Wrap the Ketchup-Stained Tablecloth Around Me

Then I slink down to the lobby
to ask Dexter for a new room key,

trying to ignore his snickering
and his bouncing Adam's apple,

and all the weird looks
the other hotel guests keep giving me . . .

When I finally
get back to my room,

I fling the tablecloth into a corner,
and grab my cell phone.

But there are
no texts from Connor.

No
voice messages.

Not
a single

missed
call.

I Sink Down

Onto the edge of the bed,
feeling as flattened
as road kill.

Then, the shrill wail
of an ambulance siren
shrieks past on the highway.

Oh *no* . . . Connor was way
too drunk to drive when he left here.
I never should have let him go!

What if
something awful
has happened to him?

What if he's had a hideous accident?
What if he's lying
in a hospital bed right now,

an oxygen mask covering his beautiful face,
his broken body hooked up
to wires and machines,

hanging
on to life
by a slim thread?

Wait a Minute . . .

This is ridiculous.
I'm really going off the deep end here.
I have got to get a grip . . .

I know what to do—I'll call him.
I'll call him and he'll pick up his phone
and then I can stop worrying, right?

I punch in his number,
then squeeze my eyes shut and wait.
But he doesn't pick up.

I text him: **R u ok?**
But he doesn't
text me back.

And I'm just about to send him
a Facebook message,
when I realize

that we aren't friends on Facebook
and that I can't friend him,
because I don't know his last name,

and that I can't go over to his house
and knock on his door,
because I don't even know

where he lives.

All at Once

I feel as if
I'm being sucked down

into a pool
of quicksand.

Because if Connor
doesn't contact me,

I might never
see him again . . .

I might never
even find out

if he survived
the ride home . . .

My Fingers Are Quaking

As I Google the name
of the nearest hospital
and dial the number
of the emergency room.

I ask the woman who answers the phone
if there've been any motorcycle accidents.
"I think there *was* one . . . ," she says.
"Hang on a minute. Let me double-check."

Omigod . . .
I gnaw on my fingernails
and stare
at the clock,

wondering
how sixty seconds
could possibly
take

so

long

to

pass . . .

Then, At Long Last

The woman gets back on the line
and says, "Sorry, honey. I was wrong.
It was a Mini Cooper."

I tell her I love her,
thank her profusely,
and hang up the phone.

But, when I lie back down on the bed,
I can feel the champagne
sloshing in my stomach,

swirling around
with all those
greasy strips of bacon I ate . . .

And I barely manage
to make it into the bathroom
before I start puking my guts out.

When I'm Finished

My stomach is as empty
as the champagne bottle
that's standing next to
the uneaten bacon burgers

and the slice of cake that room service
sent up for Connor's birthday—
sad reminders of a weekend
gone terribly wrong . . .

I don't know
if I'll ever see Connor again.
Or if it's over between us. Or what.
But one thing I *do* know is this:

I can't stand looking
at those coagulated burgers or that
stale hunk of cake for one more second.
I've got to get that table out of here!

It's a tight fit through the doorway,
but when I finally manage
to shimmy it through,
the vase of roses starts to topple.

I reach
instinctively
to grab for it,
lunging across the threshold.

And an instant later,
when I turn back around
to head into my room—
I'm just in time to see

the
door
click
shut.

Seriously?

I mean,
seriously?

I fight the urge
to bang my head against the wall.

And a little later on,
when I show up back at the front desk,

wrapped in a bacon-stained
tablecloth,

Dexter doesn't even ask me
what I want.

He just smirks
and hands me another key,

while his Adam's apple
does the hula.

When I Let Myself Back Into My Room

I hurl the tablecloth into the corner
with the other one,

yank my T-shirt on,
and hurry over to check my cell phone—

still no word
from Connor.

I grit my teeth
and punch in his number.

But it goes straight
to voice mail.

I leave him a pathetic message:
"Connor . . . Please . . . Call me . . ."

And an equally pathetic text:
Miss you . . .

Then
I climb into bed

and wait . . .
and wait . . .

and wait . . .

And I'm Still Waiting an Hour Later

Thinking that they should change
the name of this room from Love Shack
to Hate Shack,

as I lie here gazing up
at all those infuriating
golden cupids

who won't quit staring at me
and shaking their heads,
their teary eyes oozing with pity . . .

When suddenly I'm seized by an urge
to climb up the winding staircase
to the tower.

My feet feel as heavy as anchors,
but something tells me
to keep on climbing.

And when I get to the top,
and look out the little window
onto the soft green lawn below,

I see a message written
with hundreds of pink rose petals:
CONNOR LOVES COLETTE.

Okay

So
that last part—

that part about climbing up to the tower
and seeing the message written on the grass—

that part
wasn't exactly true.

But sometimes,
a girl's got to make up a story or two,

just to get through the day,
you know?

Besides, for a few seconds,
while I was coming up with it,

I could almost believe
it was real . . .

Which, Of Course, It *Wasn't*

What actually happened
was that I drifted off to sleep

and dreamed
of Connor . . .

Of going
all the way with him

and of loving
every second of it . . .

Dreamed of taking out
my purple contact lenses

and letting him see
that my eyes are hazel . . .

Dreamed that he *liked*
my hazel eyes . . .

That he kissed my eyelids
and told me how pretty I was—

pretty enough
to be a movie star . . .

When I Woke Up a Few Hours Later

I was so hungover
that my head was throbbing
like I'd been whacked with a hammer

and my tongue
was glued to the roof
of my mouth.

I raided the minibar,
guzzled some designer water,
then just sat on the couch like a zombie,

nibbling on Oreos
while staring blankly at the TV
with the sound on mute . . .

Now it's dark outside,
and I'm curled up on my bed
like a miserable question mark,

trying to nod off—
because if I can only
be with Connor in my dreams,

then all I want to do is sleep.

The Next Thing I Know

My phone's ringing!
I grab it and clutch it
to my heart.

But when I say hello,
I hear, "Hello, yourthelf.
How the heck are ya, thithter?"

And though I'm crushed that it isn't Connor,
it's hearing my brother's cheery little lisp
that makes my chest ache.

I'd give anything for a whiff
of that gummy-worm scent of his
right about now . . .

"How the heck *am* I?" I say,
trying to hide the quiver in my voice.
"I'm fab. How about you?"

"I'm fab, too," he says,
"I hooked a bath!"
"You're calling to tell me you took a bath?"

"No," he says. "I *caught* a bath.
Jack took uth fithing
and I caught a huge one!"

"Ohhhh . . . ," I say.
"You caught a *bass*.
I wish I'd been there to see you do it."

"I wish Connor
had been there, too," he says.
"It wath mega cool."

And that's when I realize
that, until just now, I hadn't thought
about how it would affect *Will*

if Connor never comes back.

Somehow I Manage

To survive
the rest of the phone call
without bursting into tears.

Even when
Will says he'll tell us *both* all about it
when he gets home.

Even when
he tells me that he loves me
almost as much as he loves fishing.

Even when
Mom gets on the phone
and right away she knows something's up.

"It's not too late to join us," she says,
her voice all concerned and sympathetic.
"Sid could bring you up here in the limo."

"Don't be silly," I say.
"Connor and I are having
the best weekend ever."

And, though it makes no sense at all,
when I hear Jack calling out to me in
the background, "We miss you, Coca Cola!"

I suddenly get
a lump in my throat
that's bigger than the state of California.

Instructions for Surviving
a Connorless Sunday

Switch from sad—
to über mad.

Switch from crave—
to rant and rave.

See red.
Pummel bed.

Stamp feet.
Repeat.

By the Time Sunset Rolls Around

I feel
like a grenade
with its pin pulled out.

I roar up the steps to the tower
and scowl down at the blank green lawn,
blinking back tears.

Then I yank my cell out of my pocket
to punch in his number—
and I *do* mean "punch."

Of course, it goes straight to voice mail.
And the message I leave for him
is short but *not* sweet:

"What the hell's the matter with you?"
Then I click off and cram my phone
deep into my pocket.

I pound back down the stairs,
rage boiling in my stomach
like battery acid.

And just as I reach
the bottom step—
my phone rings!

My Hand Dives Into My Pocket

I wrap my fingers
around my pulsating lifeline,
savoring its insistent throb.

But when I yank it out
to beg him to come right over,
it's *not* He Who Shall Not Be Named.

It's Mom.
Calling to tell me
that they'll be home in twenty minutes.

"So there's still plenty of time," she quips,
"to hide any incriminating evidence."
Then she starts chuckling.

And I force myself
to chuckle right along with her,
as I fish the silver box out of my purse

and stuff it—
and all of its unused contents—
into the trash.

Then she tells me that they want to take
Connor and me out to dinner
at the Cloud Nine Café.

"Wilson tells us Connor's terrific," she says.
"He thertainly ith!" Will shouts out
in the background.

Tears blur my vision, but I put on
my chirpiest voice and tell Mom
that I'd be happy to join them,

but that Connor can't make it because
he's visiting his grandma in the nursing home.
Just like he does *every* Sunday night.

"He brings his guitar with him," I explain,
"and sings to her and all her friends.
It's the highlight of their week . . ."

Unfortunately

On my way down
to the restaurant,

I've got to pass by Dexter
at the front desk.

He winks at me, wiggles his eyebrows,
and says, "Need a new key?"

I smile at him sweetly
and say, "Suck it."

Then I pause,
just briefly,

to watch his Adam's apple
go berserk.

I Manage to Muddle Through Dinner

And it's actually sort of a relief
to take a break from obsessing
about Connor.

Will chatters away—telling me about
all the whales they saw and the fish
they caught and the snorkeling they did.

Then,
out of the blue,
he stops and says,

"Mom duthn't think
Connor'th with hith grandma.
She thinkth you two had a fight. Ith she right?"

A split second later, he yelps
and reaches under the table to rub his shin.
"Hey!" he growls at Mom. "Why'd you do *that*?"

She doesn't answer him.
She just shoots him a you-better-
change-the-subject-right-*now*! look.

But he turns to me and says,
"If Connor wath mean to you,
I'll kick him where the thun don't shine."

And when he says this,
I don't say anything.
I just give his hand a squeeze.

Because
I'm afraid if I try to speak,
I might start blubbering.

A Silence Falls Over Our Table

It's Mom
who finally breaks it:
"We don't know what happened between
you and Connor this weekend, but . . ."

Then,
she pauses,
like she's not quite sure
what to say next.

So Jack
clears his throat
and picks up
where she left off:

"Cola honey, I think
what your mother's trying to say
is that if you feel like talking about it,
we're here to listen."

And then Will chimes in with:
"And if you *don't*
feel like talking about it,
we're here to ignore you!"

Suddenly

I'm laughing and crying
at the same time

and Mom's reaching out
to hug me

and I'm getting snot
all over her Armani sweater,

but she doesn't seem
to mind.

"I don't feel like talking about it,"
I say through my tears,

"but I can't think of three people
I'd rather be ignored by."

And when
I steal a glance at Jack's face,

he's beaming like he just
won an Oscar.

Tonight

Before
I switched off the light,

I couldn't resist leaving Connor
one final voice mail:

"Sorry about that message
I left you earlier.

I guess I was feeling
pretty pissed off.

But you don't have to worry—
I'm not gonna stalk you or anything.

In fact, if I don't hear back from you,
this is the last time I'll be calling.

Sweet dreams, Connor."

The Most Miserable Week
in the History of Weeks

Even though
Will does his seven-year-old best
to distract me every day

from the fact
that my cell phone's just sitting here,
as lifeless as a rock

(with games of Hangman
and Mad Libs and a constant stream
of knock-knock jokes),

and even though
Mom and Jack rush home
from the set every night

to help me keep
that never-ending cellular silence
from slicing me to shreds

(with dinners and movies
and scandalous tales of *Love Canoe*
film crew intrigue),

and even though
I try to convince myself
that Connor's a dick

(which he obviously *must* be, or he would
have had the decency to contact me by now
to let me know he *wouldn't* be contacting me),

I still end up
sobbing myself to sleep
every night.

It's Almost Midnight on Friday

And I'm lying here on my bed,
"celebrating" the one week anniversary
of Connor's disappearance
from the face of the earth—

just lying here,
too sad even to cry,
staring at the phone gripped in my hand,
muttering, "Ring, damn you . . . *Ring.*"

But it's just staring
right back at me
like I'm some kind
of hopelessly romantic loser.

Like if it actually had eyes
it'd be rolling them right now,
saying, "Give it up, girl.
It ain't gonna happen."

Then, In the Distance

I hear the low rumble
of a thunderstorm brewing.

But, a second later, it dawns on me
that I've heard that sound before.

And that's not thunder.
That's . . . !

It couldn't be . . .
Could it?

Man.
This is epically pathetic.

Am I so desperate
to see Connor

that I've started
hearing things now?

But when I run up the tower steps
and look out the window,

I see his motorcycle
zooming up the driveway!

You Probably Think I'm Lying
Right Now

But this isn't just
another one of my stories.

This
is really happening!

And at first,
I don't do anything.

I just watch him pull into the parking lot,
feeling like I've been zapped by a stun gun . . .

Then,
I spring into action.

The golden cupids
clap and cheer me on

as I race to the bathroom
to brush my teeth,

tear through my purse
for my brush and my gloss,

and dash to the dresser
to hunt through the chaos

for the lacy black tee
from our very first date . . .

And just as I tug it on
over my head,

there's a quiet knock
at the door.

I Whiz Over to Peek Through the Peephole

And there he is,
wearing a hat
I've never seen before—

a black knit beanie
that makes him look twice as hot
as I remember him looking

(if such
an extreme level of hotness
could possibly even exist).

He flashes
me a hopeful smile
and gives me that funny little salute of his,

as if there's no door
between us,
as if he knows I'm watching him.

But,
then again,
he probably *does* know.

Because I can feel it now,
feel it so strongly—
that wavelength thing of ours . . .

I Swing Open the Door

"Hey . . . ," he says,
his amber eyes
searching mine,

the expression in them so intense
that it feels like if I don't look away
I might burst into flames . . .

I'm not sure whether I want
to kiss him or strangle him.
So I don't do either one.

I just step aside
to let him in,
without saying a word.

He shrugs off his backpack,
then reaches in and lifts out
a red heart-shaped box.

He hands it to me
with a shy smile,
and says, "Open it."

His peace offering is corny,
but sort of endearing.
Though it pisses me off, too.

Because if Connor thinks
a fancy box of chocolates
is going to make everything all right,

he's an even bigger jerk than I think he is.

A Part of Me

Wants to hurl his gift
right at his head.

But another part of me
gets this insane urge

to open the box
and stuff my face full of candy.

Though when I lift off the lid,
I make a shocking discovery:

This isn't
a box of chocolates.

It's a box of bacon—
crisp, golden brown,

and, somehow,
still warm!

Whoa . . .

I'm so awestruck
it isn't even funny.

Though I refuse
to let it show on my face.

Connor flashes me a timid smile,
and says, "Hungry?"

But I'm not even close
to forgiving him.

So I slam the box down
on the nightstand.

Then I cross my arms over my chest,
fix him with an arctic glare, and say,

"Why did you disappear
for an entire week?

I want an explanation.
And it better be good."

Connor takes a step toward me.
I take a step back.

"There *is* an explanation," he says.
"But it's *not* good . . ."

I'm In No Mood for Riddles

"What's *that* supposed to mean?" I snap.
"It means I had to go to L.A.," he says,
"to get some tests done."

Tests . . . ?
A little shudder zips up my spine.
"What kind of tests?" I say.

"I didn't call you or text you
because I . . . I wasn't ready to tell you.
I'm *still* not ready to tell you . . ."

And when he says this,
my mouth goes drier
than dust.

"Ready to tell me what?"
He reaches for my hand
and I let him take it.

"I wasn't ready
to tell you the truth."
"The truth . . . ?" I croak.

"The truth is," he says, "it was easier
to let you think I'd dumped you,
than to tell you

I have cancer."

Cancer . . . ?

I wish I could tell you
that I'm making this up—

that it's just another one
of my lies.

I wish
I could.

But
I can't.

I Just Stand Here

Feeling . . .
Feeling nothing.

Like I've been shot through
with novocaine.

"It was in remission for a while," he says.
"But not anymore . . ."

I shake my head,
not wanting to believe him,

wanting
to turn back the clock

to the moment
before I knew

this terrible thing.

They Say the Truth Will Set You Free

But take
it from me:

The truth will lock you up
in a dungeon

and swallow
the key.

My Heart Turns Inside Out

"Oh, Connor," I whisper, "Connor . . ."
I gather him into my arms.
And we just stand here,
clinging to each other.

"The cancer was gone so long," he murmurs,
"I'd started to believe it'd never come back.
I didn't want to have to tell you.
But I couldn't stay away . . ."

He leans down and kisses me—
lightly at first,
and then as if his whole life
depends on it.

And suddenly,
I need to see his tiger stripes,
need to run my fingers over them,
bury my face in them, sob into them . . .

But
when I reach up
and lift off his hat—
he's bald!

It's Lucky I'm Such a Great Liar

Because my years of practice
have prepared me well
for this situation.

I paint an awestruck smile onto my face
and run my hands over
Connor's egg-smooth head.

"Wow . . . ," I say.
"Never thought I'd date a skinhead.
But you look kind of sexy like this."

"Yeah, right," he says with a bitter laugh,
snatching his hat out of my hands
to pull it back on.

"My hair was gonna start
fallin' out from the chemo,
so I buzzed it all off . . .

Now I look like
the poster boy
for cancer research."

He's a hundred percent right about that.
But I look him square in the eye and say,
"You're a hundred percent wrong about that."

Then I slip his hat back off, and when
I tell him that bald's a good look for him,
that it's somehow strangely masculine,

his face floods with relief.

Then He Takes Hold of Both My Hands

And tells me
that he's so sorry—
sorry for not answering my texts
and my messages.

And I tell *him*
that I'm sorrier—
for putting him through
all that stop/go/yes/no stuff.

And he tells me
that I have nothing to be sorry *for*,
that *he's* the one who should be sorry—
for pushing me further than I wanted to go.

And I tell him
not to worry about that,
not to worry
about anything

but
kicking
Cancer's
butt.

Connor's Eyes Mist Over

And he tells me
that hearing me say those words

makes him feel
sort of . . . invincible—

like
he can *do* it,

like he can win
the battle.

And then
my own eyes mist over,

and I tell him
to just shut up already

and kiss me.

A Smile Spreads Across His Face

Then he presses his lips to mine,
so sweetly, so tenderly
that I almost can't bear it.

And when we pull apart,
I find myself telling him
the whole story—

about my mother giving me the condoms,
and about how I dropped them
and was so scared he'd see them . . .

And I'm just about
to confess
that I'm still a virgin—

when I
stop
myself.

Because
that's when it dawns on me
that I'm being

totally honest with him.

I'd Love to Be Able to Report

That being honest
with Connor

makes me feel cleansed or liberated
or something like that.

But
it doesn't.

It just
makes me feel exposed—

like I've removed
every stitch of my clothes.

Though Connor Doesn't Seem to Have Noticed

His eyes are wide with astonishment.
"You got the condoms from your *mother*?
She sounds pretty awesome . . ."

"Yeah," I say
with a grudging little shrug.
"I guess she's okay."

(Mom strikes again—
he hasn't even *met* her
and already she's upstaging me.)

"*My* mother," he says,
"is anything *but* awesome."
"Really?" I say. "That bad?"

"*Worse,*" he says.
"She lied to me about how sick I was.
But my dad thought I had a right to know."

All of a sudden, there's a tornado
whirling in my chest.
"A right to know . . . what?"

"Well, my dad told me . . . he told me
that if this round of chemo doesn't work,
then there's . . . there's nothin' else they can do."

I wrap my arms around Connor
and force myself
not to cry.

"But it *will* work," I say.
"It *has* to work.
We'll *make* it work!"

Then My Lips Are on His

Tasting his fear
and his grief,

wishing I could
kiss it all away . . .

And our tongues
are swirling together

and a wave of need
is welling up in me,

carrying me off
like a riptide,

farther and farther
from shore . . .

And Now Connor's Lips Are Brushing My Ear

And he's pressing his hips
hard against mine . . .

one of his hands gripping
the small of my back . . .

the other snaking up
under my tee . . .

And now his mouth
is fusing with mine . . .

and he's moaning
soft and low . . .

moving against me . . .
oh . . .so . . .slow . . .

and I'm drowning
in Connor . . .

drowning . . .
drowning . . .

And I'm Just About to Let Go

And lose myself
completely,

when my mind clicks on,
and I find myself thinking,

But if
we sleep together,

won't that make it
even harder to bear

if the chemo doesn't . . .
if it doesn't—

But I can't even let myself *finish*
that thought.

And Now

Connor's fumbling
with the zipper on my jeans

and I'm tearing my mouth
from his.

I don't say a word.
But I don't *have* to.

Because when Connor
looks into my face

he sees that my eyes
are begging him to stop.

He lets go of me,
and growls, "Not *again* . . ."

Then His Anger Melts Away

And he looks so pained,
so stricken I can barely stand it.

He heaves
a ragged, miserable sigh,

and tells me
he's sorry,

tells me I'm just too sexy,
too damn beautiful,

tells me that when he kisses me
he gets so turned on,

so outrageously worked up
that it's almost impossible

to slam on
the brakes.

Then He Says

"It'd be such a . . . such a *relief*
to finally be able to *show* you
how I feel about you.

But not until I know for sure,
not until *you* know for sure,
that that's what you really want."

"You're amazing . . . ," I say.
"You're the amazing one," he says,
reaching out to stroke my cheek.

"And I'm worried about you . . . worried
that if we . . . if we get more involved,
it'll make it even tougher on you . . .

I mean,
if the chemo doesn't . . .
if it doesn't—"

I put a finger up to his lips.
"Don't say it," I whisper hoarsely.
"Don't even say it . . ."

He studies my face for a second, then asks,
"Are we on the same wavelength about this?"
But I'm way too choked up to speak.

All I can muster is a nod.

Connor Rests His Palms
on My Shoulders

And says that maybe, at least for a while,
until he finds out if the chemo's working,

we should make a pact
to take a break from kissing

(and from everything
that kissing leads to)

and just hold hands
with each other.

The golden cupids
are not at all pleased.

But *I* am flooded
with a weird sort of relief.

"Connor . . . ," I say. "You're being so
incredible about this, I could kiss you."

He laughs and says, "That probably wouldn't
be a good idea, under the circumstances."

"Do you think it'd be okay," I ask,
"if we hug sometimes, too?"

"Sure," he says. "As long as we aren't
lyin' down . . . or standin' up . . ."

"Or drunk . . . ," I add, "or semi-clothed."
And both of us crack up.

Then Connor reaches for my hands,
weaving our fingers together.

And when I press my forehead
against his,

a feeling of all-rightness
floods through me.

Suddenly There's a Knock

It's coming from the door
that separates Will's room from mine!
"It's okay," Connor whispers. "Answer it."
Then he ducks into the bathroom.

I swing open the door,
and there's Will, in his footie pajamas,
his cheeks as flushed as two peaches,
rubbing his eyes like he's just woken up.

"What's the matter, Will?" I say, squatting
down to brush a damp curl off his forehead.
"Nothin'," he says drowsily.
"I thought I heard voitheth . . ."

"You must have been dreaming, kiddo."
"Wait a minute . . . ," he says, sniffing the air.
"Do I thmell bacon . . . ?
I *do* thmell bacon!"

Just then, Connor walks up next to me,
his black beanie covering his bald head,
and holds out the heart-shaped box to him,
saying, "You hungry, dude?"

"Connor!" Will cries,
grabbing him around his waist.
"Hey, Will," he says, tousling his hair.
"Have you grown another couple of inches?"

"I've mithed you *tho* much," Will says.
Then he adds, "That'th a mega cool hat!"
And before Connor can stop him,
he jumps up

and grabs the beanie off his head.

Will's Mouth Drops Open

"Where'd your tiger thtripeth go?"
Connor rubs a hand over his bald head.

"Um . . . ," he says. "My stripes . . . ?"
It's clear he wasn't prepared for this.

So I leap in
to help him out.

"Is it okay," I ask Connor, "if I tell him?"
He shakes his head no.

"Aw, come on," I say gently.
"We might as well get it over with."

Connor gives me a pleading look.
But I just turn back to Will and say,

"The reason his hair is gone . . . the reason
it's gone is . . . that he caught lice.

From his little cousin.
So he decided to shave his head."

Connor Looks Relieved . . .
and Impressed

His eyes are smiling at me,
but he pretends to be annoyed.
"Why'd you have to go and tell him?"

"Oh, get over it," I say. "We've all had lice."
"We thertainly have!" Will says.
"Recently?" Connor says, looking worried.

"Nope. I wath in kindergarten. Mom shaved
my head too, but I looked much cuter
than you do when *I* wath bald."

"So, this isn't a good look for me?"
"Are you kidding?" Will says. "You look like
the pothter boy for canther rethearch."

Connor and I
exchange a quick glance,
then start laughing.

Will laughs along with us,
but looks a little suspicious.
"Guyth . . . ," he says. "It wathn't *that* funny."

After

After we tuck Will into his bed
and promise him that we'll take him
to the Mid-State Fair tomorrow,

and after I walk Connor to the door
and, instead of kissing me good night,
he just gives my hand a quick squeeze,

and after he walks out into the hall
and the door clicks shut
behind him,

I throw myself
onto my bed
and cry—

I cry until
my eyes are swollen shut
and my nose is red and raw,

until
I'm hiccupping
like a little kid,

until
I'm as empty
as a jar full of nothing.

Help! Earthquake!

My bed's shaking
like   mad! I've got   to
    get out of   here   *now!*

But, wait—
Oh, thank *God*! It's only Will,
bouncing on my bed to wake me up.

"Geez," I say. "You scared me to death."
"No I didn't," he says cheerfully.
"You're not dead."

And that's
when everything
comes flooding back—

Connor's midnight visit.
The awful news he shared.
The look in his eyes when he told me.

It all comes rushing right back at me,
slamming into my gut
with the force of a wrecking ball.

But Will's Still Bouncing Away

Bouncing up and down
in blissful ignorance,
as if my bed's a trampoline.

And I can't let him see
how demolished I feel.
Or he'll start asking questions—

questions
I'm not ready
to answer.

So I pull myself together,
then grab him
and start tickling him.

And both of us are giggling wildly
when Mom and Jack walk into the room
through the connecting door.

Mom smiles when she sees us,
but Jack pretends to be horrified.
"Unhand that child, you ruffian!" he bellows.

And I can't
help laughing at his
melodramatic performance.

"It sure is good to see you looking
so happy again, Coca Cola," he says,
beaming his movie-star smile at me.

"Oh, she'th not really that happy," Will says,
"now that Connor got lithe
and shaved hith head."

"Lice?" Mom says. "How do you know *that*?"
"Becauthe when he came over latht night,
he wath bald.

And Colette'th been
acting like she duthn't mind,
but I think it made her feel pretty thad."

Then he puts his hand on mine,
and says, "Don't worry, Colette.
Hith hair will grow back thoon."

And that's
when I totally
lose it.

Mom Takes One Look

At the tears
waterfalling down my cheeks,
and snaps into action—

asking Jack to take Will
down to the pool for a swim
so that she and I can have some "girl talk."

Will furrows his brows and says,
"Maybe I shouldn't leave . . . Connor'th
coming over thoon to take uth to the fair."

"Don't worry, Wonka," Jack says, steering
him out the door. "Your mom will call me when
he comes, and we can scoot right back up here."

As soon they're gone,
Mom sits me down on the couch,
brings over a box of tissues,

settles in beside me,
puts her arm around my shoulder,
then commands me to tell her everything—

the whole truth
and nothing *but*
the truth.

And for some strange reason
that's exactly
what I do.

I Tell Her That Connor Has Cancer

I tell her
that knowing this

makes me feel like there's
a crater in my heart.

I tell her that I've never been
so terrified before.

And then, she's crying
right along with me,

saying, "Oh, Colette.
No wonder you're so terrified.

You're in
a terrifying situation . . ."

She reaches for a tissue
and dabs at my tears.

Then she dabs at her own,
and says,

"But whatever happens,
I'll be here to help you through it.

And Will and Jack
will be too."

Sometimes
I really love my mother.

Then She Says

There's a question
she's been meaning to ask me.

But before she asks it,
she wants my promise

that I'll give her
an honest answer.

Uh oh. This does not sound good . . .
"What do you want to know?" I say,

hoping she won't notice
that I *haven't* promised.

But she gives me a look
and says, "I'm waiting . . ."

I give her
a look back.

"All right," I finally say.
"I promise."

Then she gets this real serious expression
on her face and says,

"Okay. How come you've worked so hard
to keep me from meeting Connor?"

Damn.
Why'd I have to promise?

I Take a Deep Breath

Then I blurt out the whole story—

"I told Connor
that you're Marissa Shawn's stand-in
because I knew that if he found
out who you *actually* were
he'd be all starstruck,
like everyone *always* is,
and then he'd forget about *me*,
like everyone always *does*,
and if that happened,
well if that happened
I just didn't think
I could stand it."

And what's totally strange is,
that after I tell her all this,
instead of lacing into me for lying,
she just says,
"Marissa Shawn's stand-in, huh?
I think we can work with that . . ."

She Makes a Few Fast Phone Calls

And suddenly
it's as if a magic wand
has been waved—

because thanks
to an emergency visit
from Lillian, Oscar, and Mitzi

(the miracle workers
on the *Love Canoe* crew in charge of
hair, makeup, and costumes),

Mom's famously flawless skin
has sprouted a realistic crop
of freckles,

her legendary white-blond curls
have been straightened
and pulled into a ponytail,

her renowned violet eyes
have been hidden behind
brown contact lenses,

and her notoriously huge boobs
look kind of regular-size,
somehow.

Then, just before eleven o'clock,
the brilliant trio of transformers
slips out through Will's room.

And,
a second later,
Connor knocks on my door.

I Send Him a Quick Text

Warning him
that he's about to meet my mother.
Whoa . . . , he texts back.

Mom clears her throat,
smoothes her hair,
sweeps open the door,

and, with a perfect English accent,
she says, "Come in, come in, dear boy!
You must be Connor. I'm Colette's mother."

Then she pauses
and looks over at me expectantly,
like she's waiting for a formal introduction.

"Connor, this is . . . Gertrude," I say,
coming up with her new name on the spot.
She shoots me an irritated glance.

"Well, that's my *given* name," she says,
offering him her hand, "but you can
call me . . . Greta. Everyone does."

"It's great to finally meet you, Greta."
"It's lovely to meet you, too, Connor darling.
Colette's told me so *little* about you."

And he laughs
at my mother's dumb joke,
instantly falling under her spell.

Because, apparently,
even when Marissa Shawn
isn't Marissa Shawn,

she can still
charm the pants off
every guy she meets.

But Want to Hear Something Really Weird?

Even though Connor seems to be
thoroughly enchanted by "Greta"—
it doesn't bother me.

In fact, I hate to admit this,
but seeing how well my mom
and my boyfriend are getting along

is kind of
giving me an attack
of the warm fuzzies.

Though I'm Anxious
to Head to the Fair

So I reach for my cell,
and I'm just about to phone Jack
and ask him to bring Will back up,

when I realize that if they see Mom,
they'll ask her why she's wearing
this strange costume.

Or—omigod, I should've thought of this—
Jack might call Mom "Marissa"
right in front of Connor!

I've got to head him off at the pass!
So I tiptoe into the bathroom
to call him.

"Listen," I whisper into my cell.
"It's a long story,
but Mom's wearing a disguise

and it might be
sort of awkward
if you ask her about it or if you—"

But Jack interrupts me in mid-sentence,
like he hasn't even been listening.
"Wonka and I will be there in a jiffy, Cola."

Then he clicks off.
And when I call him right back,
he doesn't pick up!

My Mind Starts Spinning So Fast
It Isn't Even Funny

How the hell
am I gonna lie my way
out of *this* one?

Then, just as I step out of the bathroom,
the door to Will's room swings open,
and he and Jack come bounding in.

When I see Jack, I practically fall over—
his world-renowned handsome face
is hidden by a beard and mustache!

Mom must have texted him
and told him the whole story
when I wasn't looking.

Will's eyes look brighter than klieg lights.
He leads Jack over to Connor and says,
"Connor, I'd like you to meet *Bruno*."

Then he gives me a secret wink, and tells Connor,
"Bruno'th the thtuntman on *Love Canoe*.
And he'th my mom'th boyfriend, too."

"Hey, Bruno," Connor says.
Jack smiles at him warmly,
and reaches out to pump his hand.

"Bruno"
must have an iron grip,
because Connor's wincing.

Then Jack, still smiling, says,
"There's only one thing you need to know—
if you hurt Colette, *I* will hurt *you*."

Connor turns pale as potatoes
and stammers, "Of . . . of course not, sir.
I would never, sir."

And I suppose
I ought to be pissed at Jack
for threatening Connor like that.

But instead, I find myself
fighting a truly bizarre urge to throw
my arms around his neck and hug him—

just like
a daughter
hugs a father.

Though, Naturally, I *Don't* Hug Him

I just give him
a playful shove, and say,
"Oh, Bruno, cut it out."

Then I give Mom a quick squeeze,
say hurried good-byes
to both of them,

and hustle Will and Connor out the door,
through the lobby, past Dexter's Adam's apple,
and into the Caddy.

At first, I'm worried
that Connor being so sick
will cast a shadow over the day.

And he *does* seem
a little preoccupied
when we first drive away.

But after a while,
Will starts singing
"Ninety-Nine Bottles of Beer on the Wall."

So I join in.
Then Connor does too.
And soon, we're all singing our hearts out,

as carefree
as a bus full of kids
on a field trip.

At the Fair

The three of us
wander the dusty grounds,
gorging on
deep-fried Oreos,

riding bumper cars
and the merry-go-round,
licking syrupy cones
of shaved-ice snow,

seeing Miss Mid-State Fair
receive her crown,
munching chocolate-covered corndogs,
we cruise around

watching fish-flipping contests
and dog shows,
barrel races,
and hog shows,

listening to trombones
and saxophones,
while monster trucks
crush motor homes . . .

And the whole time we roam
through this weird wonderland—
Connor never lets go
of my hand.

Then, in Late Afternoon

He suggests
we head over to the fairground rodeo,
and when we get there, he asks Will
if he wants to try mutton bustin'—

which, he says, is the little kid's version
of riding a bucking bronco.
Only instead of riding horses,
the kids ride sheep.

This sounds
way too dangerous to me.
But before I have a chance to say no,
Connor's signing the release form

and suddenly
Will's bouncing around
on the back of a sheep,
hanging on for dear life,

whooping and hollering
like a miniature cowboy,
looking as petrified
as he is thrilled.

He Gets Bucked Off in Eight Seconds

But when he trots back over to us,
he's waving a blue ribbon that says:
"First Place Wool Warrior."

He flings his triumphant little self
into my arms and says, "I've alwayth
wanted to win a blue ribbon!"

"Well," Connor says, slapping him five,
"then I guess you can cross that one
off your bucket list."

Will asks him what a bucket list is,
and Connor says, "It's a list of all the things
you want to do before you kick the bucket."

Will scratches his head.
"Why would I want to kick a bucket?" he says.
Connor and I exchange a suddenly sober glance.

"It's just an expression," I tell Will.
"When someone dies, you say
that they've 'kicked the bucket.'"

"Ohhhh," Will says, "Then I don't need
to make my bucket litht yet becauthe I'm not
gonna die till I'm very old, right?"

And when I answer Will's question,
I look directly into
Connor's eyes.

"That's absolutely right," I say,
"*None* of us are going to die
till we're very, *very* old."

Later

After we drop Will off
with "Greta" and "Bruno,"
we head downstairs to the Cloud Nine Café.

And as we slip into a booth,
a sign catches my eye
that I've somehow never noticed before:

EAT HERE AND BE HAPPY FOREVER.
Connor notices it too.
"'Forever . . . ,'" he says. "What a concept . . ."

He reaches up
to run a hand through his hair.
But then he stops, looking taken aback.

He shakes his head.
"Maybe it's time," he says quietly,
"for me to make *my* bucket list."

My heart contracts.
"The chemo's going to *work*, Connor.
You don't need a bucket list."

"You're probably right," he says.
"But I think I'll make one anyway.
Just in case."

"I guess it's not a bad idea," I say.
"Because, I mean, you never know—
you might get a fatal paper cut next week . . ."

"Or be bitten by a rabid teddy bear . . . ," he says.
"Or be *bored* to death," I say,
"by the ten-zillionth episode of *Survivor*. . . ."

And we come up with so many
funny ways for Connor to be killed,
that he almost dies laughing.

What I Don't Tell Him

Is that the very first thing on *my* bucket list
is to lift our ban on kissing . . .

After dinner,
when we're lying in my bed on our backs,

with only the tips
of our pinky fingers touching,

I want to kiss him so bad
my whole body aches.

"Man . . . ," Connor whispers. "I want to kiss
you so much right now it actually hurts."

"Whoa . . . ," I whisper back.
"We're doing that wavelength thing again . . ."

Then he pulls me to him,
wraps his arms around me,

and presses the length
of his body against mine.

And we just lie here like this,
totally still,

our mouths so close
I can feel his breath on my lips,

so close,
that pretty soon,

it starts to seem like
we're two bolts of lightning

with nowhere
to strike.

I'm Not Sure

How much more of this torture I can take.
So I force myself to say,

"You know, I think we're sort of breaking
the no-hugging-while-lying-down rule . . ."

Connor sighs
and says, "I guess you're right.

Maybe we should stop.
It's just makin' it *harder*."

Then he wiggles his eyebrows lewdly
and adds, "Pun intended."

Which
cracks us both up.

And after that, we somehow manage
to let go of each other

and climb
out of bed

and walk
across the room

and say
good night

without our lips
touching

even
once.

But a Few Seconds After He's Gone

There's a knock
on my door.

And when I sprint back over
and look through the peephole,

Connor's
standing there—

holding up a piece of paper that says
To heck with the ban on kissing.

My heart
flies into the stratosphere.

I yank open the door,
tug him inside,

wrap my hands
around the back of his neck

and cover his lips
with mine.

So Sue Me

Everything
on that last page

was pure
fabrication—

just little old me
doing my reinventing reality thing.

But there's no law against
a girl making up stories.

And I sure am lucky
there *isn't*.

Or I'd be serving
a life sentence by now.

On Sunday Morning

I wake up wishing more than anything
that Connor and I could spend
the whole day alone together,
the whole *week* alone together . . .

And half an hour later
my wish comes true,
when he shows up
and pops a brochure into my hand—

a brochure for a day camp at the zoo
for "junior zookeepers in training."
A camp that starts tomorrow morning
and lasts for seven whole days.

The golden cupids cry, "Yes!"
and pump their chubby little fists in the air.
I fling my arms around Connor's neck
and tell him he's my hero.

Then we rush next door
to tell Will about it,
who starts bouncing up and down
like a human pogo stick,

shouting,
"Mega cool! Mega *mega* cool!"
Connor flashes me a heart-stopping grin,
then locks eyes with me and whispers,

"Mega mega *mega* cool . . ."

I Use My Calculator App
to Figure It Out

Seven days
equals 168 hours.

168 hours
equals10,080 minutes.

10,080 minutes
equals 604,800 seconds.

604,800 seconds,
plus one Connor and one me,

minus one Will—
equals 604,800 seconds

of ecstasy!

Okay

So I know that sounded
a little delirious.

I mean, obviously,
Will won't be gone every single second.

But he *will* be gone
all day long.

And when I tell Mom and Jack
that I want to use the time

to help Connor do everything
on his bucket list,

they volunteer to babysit every night,
and on the weekend, too.

Sometimes,
I guess it pays to tell the truth.

On Monday Morning

As soon as Sid heads off with Will
to drive him to camp,
I text Connor to come right over.

But when he gets here
a few minutes later,
and gives me that funny little salute,

I'm struck by
how incredibly tired he looks.
And how terribly sick.

And is it just my imagination,
or are his clothes starting to look
a little baggy on him?

I feel
the fear rising in me
like a black tide,

but I shove it back down,
and force myself to focus
on his eyes instead.

They're so full of . . . I don't know . . .
life, I guess . . . and of something else, too . . .
Mischief, maybe?

His hairless head is hidden
under a dove grey fedora
from like the 1950s or something.

"Awesome hat," I say.
"Makes you look sort of like a mobster.
All you need now is a machine gun."

"Yeah," he says,
"a machine gun, a bucket list,
and a dame like you by my side."

The Week Whooshes By

Kind of like the view out the window
from a train that's taking you everywhere
you ever dreamed of going.

We go hang gliding.
And kayaking.
And learn how to juggle.

We hike
into the middle of the woods
and scream at the top of our lungs.

We sneak
into someone's backyard
and steal a midnight swim in their pool.

We walk
into an ice-cream shop and buy
triple-scoop cones for all the customers.

We stand under a waterfall.
Send a message in a bottle.
See a meteor shower.

And with each day that passes,
when it's time to say good night,
it takes more and more willpower

not to wrap my arms around Connor,
not to press my lips
to his.

I Never Knew

That there were
so many ways

for two people
to hold hands—

so
many

tempting,
seductive,

feverishly
flirty ways

for
five fingers

to
entwine

with
mine.

Today Is Will's Last Day of Camp

Our
freedom
is coming to an end.

Connor was so exhausted from
our whirlwind week of bucketlisting,
that he had to sleep in.

And when
he finally showed up
on his motorcycle a couple of minutes ago

and whisked me away
to take a ride in a hot air balloon
(the last thing left on his list),

I couldn't help noticing that
the shadows under his eyes
seemed even darker,

even deeper
than they were
just yesterday . . .

But as we cruise
up the Coast Highway to Paso Robles
for our balloon ride,

I decide not to think
about any of that.
I decide not to think

at all . . .

Connor and I

Drift through
the sky,

floating above
the soft straw hills,

the dollhouse towns,
the toy-car streets . . .

We skim along
on our windblown retreat

as sunset catches
the clouds on fire.

And it's only through
an act of will,

while we hover over
the world like this,

that I manage
not to give in to desire

and give him
a toe-curling soul-scorching

kiss.

We're Back in San Luis Obispo Now

Sitting on a bench
in the very same park where Will first
introduced us to each other.

Just sitting here,
watching the full moon rise
over the sycamores.

Was it really only a month ago?
So much has happened since then.
And so much hasn't . . .

Connor's arm
is around my shoulder,
his thigh barely grazing mine,

but all the atoms in my body
are yearning to merge
with all the atoms in *his*.

His fingers
slip off my shoulder,
and swirl up to my earlobe,

setting
all my earrings tinkling
and my nerve endings firing . . .

"You hungry?" he says.
"Famished," I murmur.
Though *food*'s the furthest thing

from my mind . . .

Connor Stands Up

"Come with me," he says.
"I'm takin' you out to dinner."

As we stroll toward the parking spot
where we left his motorcycle,

Connor stops to point out a big clock
mounted on a post in front of the courthouse,

and says, "I used to think that clock
was cheesy. But not anymore . . ."

I look up
at its big round face.

"See those words," he says,
"engraved across the bottom?"

I hadn't noticed them at first,
but now I look more closely

and read them aloud:
"Spend some time with someone you love."

"That's what I've *been* doin',"
he whispers in my ear.

I turn and fall into his amber eyes.
"Me too," I whisper back.

And when he hears my words,
he looks so happy and so sad,

so beautiful, but so pale and sick,
that I just can't fight it anymore—

I pull him to me
and press my lips to his.

We Throw Ourselves

Into
the abyss
of the kiss,

pouring
seven days
of pent-up passion,

of every
opportunity
missed,

into this sudden
sizzling starburst
of bliss . . .

When We Finally Manage to Stop

Both of us are breathing so hard
it isn't even funny.

I shrug and say, "Oops."
Connor laughs.

"I'd have kissed *you*," he says,
"if you hadn't kissed me first."

He still has those awful
dark shadows under his eyes,

but there's some color
in his cheeks again—

like we're in some weird
backwards fairy tale or something,

and the maiden's kiss
has brought the prince back to life.

"Do you ever get the feelin'," he says,
"that we're livin' in a sort of . . .

a sort of reverse version
of *Sleepin' Beauty*?"

My jaw drops open.
"Unbelievable . . . ," I murmur.

"What?" he says. "Did we just do that wavelength thing again?"

"Boy," I say.
"Did we *ever*."

Then We Climb Onto His Bike

I wrap myself around him
and we zoom up the street

until we come to a sign that says
WELCOME TO THE APPLE FARM INN.

"This is it," Connor says.
"An inn . . . ?" I say.

"Yeah. There's a restaurant here
that serves the best bacon quiche ever."

He holds the door open for me,
in that adorable old-school way of his,

and leads me to the quietest corner
of the dining room.

We slip into a cozy booth for two,
lit by a stained glass lamp.

Connor glances
at the wall next to our table.

I look up too,
and see an old-fashioned poster—

a picture of two lovers
looking up at a full moon.

Suddenly, I Get All Choked Up

I turn to look back at Connor,
and he seems choked up too.
He takes hold of my hands,
gripping them tightly in his.

"Life *is* good," he says.
"Especially the time I've spent with you.
But it's just that I'm not . . .
I'm not . . ."

Then his voice cracks
and he looks down at the table.
Dread seeps into the pit of my stomach.
"You're not . . . what?" I manage to croak.

Connor looks back up at me and says,
"I'm not sure . . . I'm not sure
how much more time we'll *have* . . .
How much more time I've *got* . . ."

"You've got tons of time," I say.
"The chemo's going to *work*."
Connor sighs a long, bleak sigh.
"That's the thing," he says quietly.

"It didn't."

And, under them,
just three words:

"Life is good."

This Can't Be Happening . . .

Connor's telling me
that he found out
yesterday.

But that he just couldn't
bring himself
to break the news to me,

couldn't
bring himself
to let me know

that he has to leave
for L.A. tomorrow
to go back into the hospital

so that
his doctors can try
an experimental treatment—

the kind
they only try
when everything else

fails.

My Chest Feels Like It's Splitting in Two

My eyes
blur with tears,

but I *will* them
not to fall.

I reach out
to stroke Connor's cheek

and tell him that the experimental treatment
is going to cure him.

I tell him
I'm absolutely sure of it.

Though, of course, I'm *not* sure.
Not sure at all . . .

Then All of a Sudden

The waitress is here—smiling down at us
with her pad and pencil poised.

"You two lovebirds
ready for some dinner?"

The question snaps Connor
out of his somber state.

"Some bacon quiche for m'lady?" he asks.
I nod, and he orders it for each of us.

Then, as the waitress waddles away
from our table,

he leaps up, taps her on the shoulder,
and whispers something in her ear.

She winks at him
and heads off toward the kitchen.

He slides back
into the booth and says,

"Well, *some*one had to tell her
it's your birthday."

I Laugh and Take Hold
of His Hands Again

Connor smiles
a wistful smile,
and says,

"I know this might sound sappy,
but this last week with you,
this whole summer with you,

has made me feel . . . I don't know . . .
made me feel ready, I guess . . .
for what*ever* happens."

I try to speak,
but the lump in my throat
won't let me.

"I mean, we've done almost everything
on my bucket list, right?" he says
with a bittersweet laugh.

"*Almost* everything?" I say hoarsely.
"Wasn't riding in a hot air balloon
the last thing on your list?"

"Well," he says,
lacing our fingers together.
"To be honest . . ."

Then he hesitates,
searching my eyes.
"There *is* one *more* thing . . ."

And, somehow,
I know what it is
before he even whispers it:

"I want to spend the night with you."

Connor's Cheeks Flush

"That is…
if you *want* me to . . .

Of course, I'll totally understand
if you—"

But I don't
even let him finish his sentence.

I just
lean across the table

and
kiss him—

deeply, deliberately,
decisively.

And When We Pull Apart

Connor looks
so moved . . . so gorgeous . . .
so completely thrilled,

that I can't resist
leaning right back in
and kissing him again—

kissing him
with everything
I've got.

"Let's stay here tonight,"
he murmurs breathlessly.
"Let's get a room right now."

"Will they let us?" I say.
"Neither of us is twenty-one."
"I've got a fake ID," he says.

Then he throws some money
onto the table for the waitress,
tugs me up out of the booth,

and ten miraculous minutes later
he's slipping the key into the door
of room 317.

We Step Into the Dimly Lit Room

And even before the door
closes behind us,
Connor's lips find mine—

and he's kissing me softly,
so softly . . . softly . . .
over and over again . . .

kissing my lips . . .
my ears . . . my neck . . .
my shoulders . . .

till my heart's
beating faster than
a hummingbird's wings . . .

And Now

He's inching me back,
pressing me against the wall,

leaning his whole body
into mine,

his hands slipping behind me
to grip my hips,

pulling them
toward his,

easing one of his thighs
between mine,

his every move
rippling through me

till I'm dizzy, buzzing,
trembling . . .

And Then My Knees Are Buckling

And I'm grabbing onto Connor's arms
to steady myself, saying, "Whoa . . .
I think I better sit down."

"You okay?"
"Yeah. But you've got to
stop making me swoon like this."

Connor laughs and leads me over to the bed.
"We never did have dinner," he says
reaching into his backpack.

"You probably just need
somethin' in your stomach.
I brought us a little homemade snack."

He pulls out a baggie full of brownies.
"You *baked* those?" I say.
"Especially for you," he says.

Then he takes one of them out,
holds it up to my lips,
and feeds me the first bite.

It's Dense and Sweet and Rich

With a hint of something earthy in it . . .
Coffee maybe?

"This tastes awesome," I say,
licking the crumbs off my lips.

He leans in for another kiss.
"*You* taste awesome," he says.

He flicks on the fake fire in the fireplace,
swings open the fridge,

pulls out a couple of beers and says,
"Let's wash the brownies down with these."

And for a while we just sit here,
facing each other on the bed,

our legs crossed,
our knees touching,

swigging our beers
and kissing . . .

nibbling our brownies
and kissing some more . . .

"Do you feel a buzz yet?" he asks.
"I've only had half a beer . . . ," I say.

"True," he grins. "But you've also had half
a brownie—baked with a secret ingredient."

"A secret ingredient?"
"Yeah," he says."Medical marijuana—

the only perk
of having cancer."

I Stare Down at the Brownie in My Hand

And the reality
of what's happening
begins to dawn on me.

"No *wonder*
eating it was only
making me *hungrier* . . ."

And then,
I start laughing—
because somehow

this is
the most hilarious thing
that's ever happened to me,

the most hilaaaaarrrrrious thing
that's ever happened to anyone
in the history of the universe . . .

And Connor's Laughing Too

Leaning in for beery kisses . . .
And brownie kisses . . .

And then—
neither of us is laughing.

And he's lifting the brownie
and the beer out of my hands,

easing me back
against the pillows,

telling me how long he's waited
for this to happen,

telling me
how amazing it's gonna feel,

telling me he's never
wanted anything more

in his whole entire
life . . .

And Then

We're
kissing again—

kissing
each other

into
oblivion . . .

And That's When I Hear It—

The ticking of the massive clock
above the mantel.

And once I *start* hearing it—
tic . . . tic . . . tic . . .

I can't *stop* hearing it—
tic . . . tic . . tic . . .

Can't stop thinking
about the fact

that our first time together—
tic . . . tic . . . tic . . .

might also be
our last.

And my heart
dissolves in my chest,

washing away like a sand castle
built too close to shore.

I Rip My Lips From Connor's

And cup his face
in my hands.

His eyes are soft
and gleaming,

but those shadows under them
seem darker than ever.

They make him look so weary,
so deathly ill . . .

I rub the pads of my thumbs
across them a few times,

wishing
I could just erase them.

And then,
with a sudden gut-wrenching

jolt—

I
realize

that
I *can*!

But That's Not Possible . . .

Is it . . . ?
I shake my head,
trying to grasp
what I'm seeing.

"This is crazy . . . ," I murmur.
"I must be way more stoned than I thought.
I must be hallucinating . . ."
"What makes you say that?" Connor says.

He's got the strangest look
in his eyes all of a sudden—
like he's handling a bomb
that might explode any second.

"The shadows under your eyes," I whisper.
"They rubbed off . . ."
"No they didn't, babe . . . ," he says.
"That's just the weed talkin'."

But then his eyes dart to my hands.
And when I follow his gaze,
I see that the pads of my thumbs
are blackened and smudged—

as if I've been handling mascara . . .

I Stare at Them Dumbly

Trying to wrap my head
around what's happening.
"Those shadows . . . ," I say.
"Those shadows weren't *real*?"

Connor hesitates,
his eyes flitting around the room
like he's looking for the nearest
emergency exit.

Then he says,
"You're . . . you're too stoned . . .
Those brownies were . . . they were potent . . .
They're puttin' crazy thoughts in your head."

His voice sounds so soothing,
but a little trembly, too,
as if he's trying to talk me down
off a ledge.

"You're thinkin' too much, girl," he says,
tapping me gently on my forehead.
"Don't think. Just feel . . ."
Then he leans in to kiss me again.

But I say, "Wait . . . I don't get it . . .
Why would you want
to make yourself look even worse
if you're so incredibly sick?"

He doesn't answer me.
He just turns away
and stares into the fireplace
at the fake flames . . .

And Now

The truth
begins sinking into me—

sinking in
like a slow-motion ax

hitting me right between
the eyes.

"Wait a minute . . .
Maybe you're *not* incredibly sick.

Are you even sick
at *all* . . . ?"

For a Split Second

Connor's eyes widen.
Then he bursts out
laughing,

and wipes away
the beads of sweat on his forehead
with the back of his hand.

"Man . . . ," he says,
"Sounds like that weed
made someone a little paranoid."

He reaches out to ruffle my hair
and says, "You gotta chill, babe.
You *really* gotta chill."

Then he hops out of bed
and goes over to examine his face
in the mirror above the desk.

"Weird . . . ," he says,
shooting me a quick uneasy glance.
"Those shadows *do* look a little lighter . . ."

He keeps on talking.
But I can't hear
what he's saying.

Because there's a drumming in my ears now,
a drumming that's getting louder
and louder and…

No way . . . No *way*!
He fooled me with the same trick
I've used on my mother a zillion times?

The old
mascara-under-the-eyes-
to-make-yourself-look-sick trick!

I Heave Myself Up From the Bed

And lurch across the room,
till we're standing
so close

that I can see
the muscle twitching
under his left eye.

"Why don't you just admit it?" I scream.
Connor's expression goes strangely blank.
"Admit what?" he says.

"Admit that your whole story
about having cancer
was just a big huge steaming pile

of bullshit!"

Connor Opens His Mouth to Speak

But
no words
come out.

The color drains
from his cheeks so fast,
it's like someone pulled a plug.

He takes a step back,
holding up his hands like he's trying
to calm a rabid dog.

"Hang on . . . Take it easy,"
he says with a choked little laugh.
"That's *good* news, right? I'm not sick."

"Oh yes you are!
You're the sickest bastard
I've ever met!"

And That's When

I'm catapulted
into an epically psycho
moment—

because
I'm thrilled to know
that Connor's not dying.

But I wish
the scumbag
was dead.

I Take a Step Forward

And slam
the palms of my hands
into his chest.

He reels back, caught off-balance.
And, for a second, he looks like
he's going to shove me right back.

But instead,
he reaches up to tear at his hair,
then growls when he remembers he's bald.

"Jesus . . . ," he mutters to himself.
"All that effort . . . right down the drain . . .
I was this close . . . *this* close . . ."

"This close . . . to what?" I whisper.
But my heart shrivels,
because I already know the answer.

Connor Doesn't Say Anything

He just jams his hands
into his pockets and shoots
an angry glance at the bed.

Then he turns back to me
with a desperate,
almost pleading look in his eyes.

"I was this close," he says,
"to finally being able . . .
to *show* you how I *feel* about you."

"Omigod . . . ," I say.
"That's why you shaved
your head?

That's why
you put that mascara
under your eyes?

To make yourself look
so sick that I'd believe
you had terminal cancer?

So sick that I'd take pity on you
and grant a 'dying man'
his *last wish*?

You asshole, you!
You did all this
just to get into my pants?"

Connor Looks Hurt

"You gave me no choice," he says.
"I wanted you so bad . . .
I still do."

I can't breathe.
My lungs feel like they're crammed
with shards of shattered glass.

I stumble over to the couch,
and sink into the farthest corner of it,
hugging my knees to my chest.

"But how could you have lied
about a thing like that?
About *dying*, for chrissake?"

Connor gives me a proud little smirk.
"Lying's what I do," he says with a shrug.
"I'm kind of famous for it.

My friends call me 'The Conman.'"

"'The Conman' . . . ?"

"At your service," he says.
Then he gives me
that funny little salute of his.

I used to think
it was kind of cute when he did that.
But not anymore.

"Quit saluting me!" I yell.
"Why are you always *doing* that?"
The smirk slips from his face.

"I was an army brat," he says.
"Every time we moved to a new base,
I got beat up by a fresh crop of punks.

But then I figured out
that if I lied to them,
I could keep that from happening.

I'd just tell 'em my dad was a general.
Or that I had a knife and I knew how to use it.
I got real good at lying, real fast."

"But . . . but I thought . . .
I thought you couldn't lie your way
out of a paper bag," I say.

"That was all just part of my act.
Guess you fell for it, huh?
You were so easy to fool . . ."

"Easy . . . to fool?" I say.
"Yeah," he says. "But somehow,
that just made me want you even more.

There was something sort of . . .
I don't know . . . sort of sexy, I guess,
about how gullible you were."

"Gullible . . . ?" I say. "A couple
of hours ago, when you and I stood
in front of that clock . . .

When we stood there
and you told me you'd been spending time
with someone you love—

I didn't know
you meant
yourself!"

Connor Grabs His Heart

And staggers back,
pretending to be wounded.
"Ouch," he says. "You *got* me."

Suddenly,
there's a swarm of killer bees
buzzing through my veins.

"What else have you lied to me about?"
"Oh . . . ," he says. "This and that . . ."
"Give me a for instance," I say.

"Okay . . .
I'm a tad older than I told you I was."
"*How* old?"

"I'm twenty-one."
Holy shit . . . Twenty-freaking-one . . . ?
"So even your *fake ID* was fake?" I say.

"Yeah," he says with a wry smile.
"Pretty ironic, right?"
I nod grimly.

"And I suppose it wasn't
actually your birthday, was it," I say,
"that night we drank the champagne?"

"Nope," he says. "But look who's
talkin'—it's *your* birthday every time
you walk into a restaurant."

"Maybe so," I roar.
"But all *I'm* trying to get
is a piece of cake!"

He laughs and says,
"What's the difference?
Piece of cake, piece of ass . . ."

A Hurricane Rips Through Me

"That's all I am to you?" I shout.
"A piece of ass?"
"Of course not," he says.
"I was just kiddin' . . ."

He flops down
on the other end of the couch
and says, "I like you. I like you a lot.
More than any girl I've ever known."

If looks could kill, Connor would be dead.
"I *do*," he says. "Why else would I have gone
to all this trouble? You should feel flattered."
"Flattered . . . ?"

"Sure," he says. "I mean, most girls,
if I spent a couple of weeks with 'em
and they wouldn't do it with me,
I'd have been out of there."

His amber eyes are gleaming now,
catching the fake fire's flicker.
"But you—you're different," he murmurs.
"I'm kind of obsessed with you . . ."

He slides a little closer to me
and the moonlight streams onto his face
through the shutters at the window,
casting thin stripes of light across it.

And that's when I realize
that, even without his hair,
Connor looks exactly like a tiger—
a tiger who's stalking

his prey!

Every Muscle in My Body Tenses

"You know," he says,
"you're sort of irresistible."

Then he slides
even closer to me.

"I've been with dozens
of other girls.

But I've never wanted anyone
more than I want you."

"If you were so desperate to sleep with me,
why'd you ask for that ban on kissing?"

"It worked on another girl once," he says.
"Got her so horny she finally put out.

It worked on you, too, didn't it, babe?
You want it just as much as I do . . ."

A Shiver Runs Through Me

I want to leap up from the couch
and run out of the room.

But it's like I've been paralyzed . . .
Or hypnotized . . .

Omigod . . .
Omi*god* . . .

Connor locks eyes with me
and slides closer still,

till he's only
a few inches away.

"I mean,
it'd be *so* awesome . . . ," he says.

Then he laughs to himself
and shakes his head.

"Though my friends
would never believe me.

They'd just think it was more
of The Conman's usual BS.

But *I'd* know.
I'd know that I'd made it

with Marissa Shawn's daughter."

A Stick of Dynamite

Has just
blasted apart

my
heart.

When I Finally Manage to Get a Grip

I ball up my fists,
stare him coldly in the eye, and hiss,
"Marissa Shawn *isn't* my mother."

"Oh, get real," he says.
"I recognized her that first day, when I
rode up next to your car on my bike."

"Sorry to disappoint you," I growl.
"But do you honestly think Marissa Shawn
would be caught dead driving a Prius?"

Connor blinks in bewilderment.
"But . . . but I thought you were lyin'," he says.
"I thought Greta was Marissa in disguise."

"Well, you thought wrong," I snap.
"All this whole time, you've been
trying to nail the stand-in's daughter."

A Steely Look Comes Into His Eyes

He wraps his hands around my upper arms
and eases me up from the couch,
till we're standing face to face.

"Please, baby . . . ," he says,
"I don't care *who* your mother is.
It's *you* I want."

He's holding my arms
so tight now,
it almost hurts.

"Have a heart," he says.
"I've spent all summer
tryin' to make this happen . . ."

A sliver of moonlight falls into his eyes—
and that's when I notice.
"You're . . . you're wearing *contacts*!" I gasp.

For a second,
Connor looks rattled.
Then he shakes it off.

"I am?" he says,
pretending to be shocked. "I *wondered*
what those things floatin' in my eyes were . . ."

And then
he snickers
at his own lame joke.

This Is All Too Much . . .

"What's your true eye color?" I whisper.
"I guess the jig is up," he says.
"They're brown."

"That's because you're so full of *shit*," I snarl.
He clenches his jaw
and tightens his grip on my arms.

"Come on," he says,
"that's not how you really feel, is it?
Think of everything I've done for you.

Think of
everything I've sacrificed.
I shaved my freakin' head for you.

I even
put up with
that bratty little brother of yours . . ."

My breath catches in my throat.
"Don't you think it's time," he says,
"to give me what I deserve?"

I look into his treacherous face for a second.
Then I slap on a flirty smile,
and say, "I thertainly do."

Connor laughs,
and his whole being
seems to light up with relief.

Then
he leans in
to kiss me.

But just before
his lips meet mine—
I snap my knee up into his crotch.

He groans,
grabs himself,
and crumples to the floor.

I snatch my things, rush to the door,
and when I slam it shut behind me,
it feels like I'm slamming it shut

on
everything
that's happened this summer.

I Careen Down the Long Hallway

Then
turn a corner,

and stop
short

at the sight
of my own reflection

staring back at me
from a big round mirror—

my hair,
wild and disheveled,

my face,
pale as fog,

my eyes,
wide and purple . . .

So
purple . . .

My Blood Freezes

Connor's
not the only one

who's been
wearing contacts . . .

He's not
the only one

who's lied about his age
or his birthday . . .

He's not
the only one

who's rubbed mascara
under his eyes

to trick someone
into thinking he was sick!

I Turn Away From the Mirror

And dash down the stairs,
through the lobby,
and out into the night.

I sprint past the restaurant,
streak through the parking lot,
and run down the sidewalk.

I run
as if I'm running
for my life—

my heart hammering,
my breath coming in short sharp gasps,
the stitch in my side knifing into me.

But no matter
how much distance I put
between Connor and me,

I can't escape
the awful
truth:

I'm
just
like

him.

No Wonder . . .

No
wonder

we've always been
on the same wavelength.

The Conman
and me—

we're two lying peas
in a pod.

A Wave of Nausea Crashes Over Me

I skid to a stop
and pitch forward,

retching up
beer and brownie and bile,

and the bitter aftertaste
of every lie Connor told me,

and of every lie
I told *him*,

and of all the lies
I've ever told *any*one . . .

I retch
and retch and retch

until there's nothing left
inside of me

but a terrible
aching clarity—

I have got to stop
lying.

I've got to stop
today.

Right this
very instant.

I've got to stop
while I still

can.

I Pull Out My Cell and Call My Mother

"Mom," I say, trying to keep
the wobble out of my voice,
"can you come get me?"

"What's the matter, honey?" she says.
"Nothing," I say. "It's just that Connor had . . .
he had a family emergency and he had to—"

Oh, damn. *Damn* . . .
I'm doing it again,
aren't I?

"No, wait," I say. "That's not true, Mom.
I'll tell you . . . I'll tell you the truth
when you get here."

Man . . .
This is going to be a lot harder
than I thought.

Ten Minutes Later

I see
Jack's Porsche
rounding the corner.

Aw, geez . . . Why'd Mom send *him*?
Why couldn't she just come
to get me herself?

But when the car pulls over to the curb,
Jack's not the only one who steps out of it—
Mom and Will do too.

And I guess I must look pretty bad,
because Will races right over to me
and asks me why I'm so sad.

"I'm not sad," I say, "I'm just . . ."
Oh, for *chrissake*.
There I go *again*.

"Wait," I say, holding up my hand.
"That's not true, Will. I *am* sad.
I'm freaking miserable."

And all of a sudden
I'm crying harder
than I've ever cried in my life.

"If your heart's been broken," Jack says,
"we're here to help you put it back together."
And the three of them wrap me into a group hug.

Which is totally corny,
but somehow totally awesome
at the same time.

After I Run Out of Tears

And they whisk me back to the hotel,
and Mom fills the bathtub
with bubbles for me,

and Jack brews me a cup of chamomile tea,
and Will draws me a picture
of a monkey,

I finally tell them that Connor was
lying to me about being sick.
The golden cupids frown and shake their fists.

Mom's hand flies up to her mouth.
"Why the hell would he lie about
a thing like that?" she says.

Jack's eyes flash.
"Yeah," he says. "What possible reason
could that kid have had?"

Will furrows his brows.
"Why would he tell you he had lithe
if he didn't have lithe?"

I don't want to lie,
but I don't want to corrupt
my baby brother either.

So I choose my words carefully.
"Connor told me an even worse lie than that.
He told me he was very, very sick.

He *did* that because he wanted something . . .
something that . . .
that belonged to me . . .

And he thought that if he told me
he was really sick, I'd feel so sorry for him
that I'd be more willing to give it to him."

Will cocks his head to the side.
"I'm thinking that thith ith either
about bacon . . . or about thex.

Am I right?"

And Suddenly, I'm Laughing

And then Mom and Jack are laughing too.
Will looks pleased with himself,
but confused.

"What'd I thay . . . ?" he asks.
"Nothing," I say.
"We're not laughing at *you*."

But as soon as the words
pop out of my mouth,
I realize I'm lying again.

"Wait," I say.
"I guess we *are*
laughing at you.

Though only because . . .
because you sound so . . .
so grown-up for your age."

"I thertainly do!" he crows.
And, all at once, I remember
my last words to Connor.

And
my laughter
morphs into tears.

All Weekend Long

I weep.
Sleep.
Try to eat.

Curse.
Sigh.
Admit defeat.

Toss. Turn.
Simmer.
Burn.

Rant.
Rave.
Repeat.

Late Sunday Afternoon

I wake up from yet another nap,
and find Will sitting
on the edge of my bed.

He hands me an Oreo and a tissue.
"Feeling any better?" he says.
I just honk my nose and shrug.

"When I think about what that athwipe
did to you," he says, "I feel furiouth."
I offer him a weak smile.

"When *I* think about
what that asswipe did to me,
I feel pathetic."

"Well," he says,
folding his arms across his chest,
"what are you gonna do about that?"

His question
swirls around my head
like a mist . . .

What *am* I gonna do about that?

Then

Out of nowhere,
the answer just sort of pops
into my mind.

I leap out of bed,
pump my fist
into the air,

and say, "I'll *tell* you
what I'm gonna do about it—
I'm gonna get revenge!"

And
suddenly I feel
like my homeless heart

has just found
a new place
to live.

Revengeville

The plan comes to me,
fully formed,

in one of those electrifying bolts
of inspiration—

I'm gonna teach The Conman
a lesson he'll never forget.

I'm gonna give him a taste
of his own freaking medicine.

Only, instead of faking
being terminally ill,

I'm gonna take it
a step further than he did.

A giant step
further:

I'm gonna fake
my own death.

When I Tell Will My Idea

He high-fives me and shouts,
"That'th what I'm talkin' about!"

Then he begs me to let him
fake *his* death, too.

So I say, "Why not?
The more corpses the merrier!"

Then we start brainstorming ideas
for how we'll kick the bucket.

We consider drowning.
(Not messy enough.)

Dismemberment by serial killer.
(Way *too* messy.)

Choking on gummy worms.
(Guess whose idea *that* was?)

And we finally opt for being
run over by a drunk driver.

It's got everything—
blood, guts, drama, the works.

The Next Few Days

Are a whirlwind
of planning, plotting,
and scheming.

When we tell Jack our idea,
he says it's brilliant, and offers
to play the part of the drunk driver.

When we tell Mom, she says,
"I'll dress up as Greta again,
and sob over your mangled corpses!"

We arrange for some of the movie extras
to play the paramedics, the cops,
and the horrified onlookers.

We put in calls
to Lillian, Oscar, and Mitzi,
who say they'll pitch in too—

promising to do hair,
makeup, and costumes
for the entire "cast."

And when we ask
the guys in the prop department
for their help,

they agree to loan us
an SUV, an ambulance,
and even a police car.

It takes
a village to get
revenge.

By Wednesday Night

Will and I have hammered out
every last detail of our scam.

We've scheduled our "deaths"
to happen on Sunday,

so that all the members of the film crew
will be available to help us.

We'll wait till nine p.m.,
when it's dark outside,

so it'll be easier to create the illusion
that an accident has happened.

"There'th only one problem," Will says.
"What?" I say.

"How do you know you can get Connor
to show up at the hotel on Thunday night?"

"Oh, don't you worry," I say.
"I've got that one covered."

On Thursday Afternoon

I begin reeling The Conman in,
with a text—

humbly apologizing for kneeing him
in the you-know-whats.

He doesn't text me back.
But I wasn't expecting him to.

Then, on Thursday night,
I text him again—

**I don't blame u
for being mad.**

**But I hope u can forgive me,
because I can't stop thinking about u.**

And this time he nibbles at the bait.
Just like I figured he would.

Really? he texts back.
Really, I reply.

And that's
no lie.

On Friday Morning

I send him another text—
telling him that I've been
trying my best to forget him,

but that I'm starting
to miss him so bad
it isn't even funny.

He doesn't answer.
But that's okay.
I didn't think he would . . .

I wait
till it's almost midnight
before I text him again—

to tell him that not seeing him
is beginning to make me feel like
an addict going through withdrawal.

He nibbles again, right on schedule,
answering my text with one of his own:
Got Connor cravings, huh?

I want u more than bacon, I reply.

On Saturday Morning

I call his cell.
He doesn't pick up.
So I leave him a message.

I make my voice
sound all breathy and sexy
and Marilyn Monroe-y,

telling him that I don't know
how much longer I can go on
without seeing him.

He doesn't
call me back.
But I'm not at all surprised.

I mean, now that I know
what makes this loser tick,
his moves are as see-through as Saran Wrap.

And it's obvious that he's just
playing hard to get because he thinks
it'll make me want him even more.

On Saturday Afternoon

I try phoning The Conman again.
And—big shock, right?—
it goes straight to voice mail.

So I put on
my Marilyn voice
again,

and tell him that I'm beginning
to think I made a big mistake
when I turned down his . . . offer.

Which is when he nibbles at my bait
for the third time,
with another text:

**U shouldn't
say things like that
unless u really mean them.**

My thumbs
zoom over the keys:
I meant every single word.

I Make a Point
of Not Calling Him That Night

And I don't call him
on Sunday morning either.

I keep him waiting
till Sunday afternoon.

Late
Sunday afternoon.

Then I dial his number.
And this time, he picks up.

Though not till like the tenth ring.
Just to make me squirm.

"I can't wait any longer," I say.
"I've got to see you tonight."

"You've '*got* to' see me?" he says
with a mocking laugh. "Why?"

"Because . . . I want to make
your wildest dreams come true."

He hesitates before answering.
Then he says, "*All* of them?"

"Every . . . last . . . one," I say.
And I can hear him suck in a thrilled breath.

"I knew you'd see the light," he says,
in this revoltingly cocky tone.

"I'll text you around nine," I say.
"As soon as I'm done babysitting Will."

"Tonight," he says,
"is gonna be life changin', babe."

"I can't wait," I purr.
Then I hang up and chuckle to myself.

If he only knew *how* life changing . . .

At Seven p.m.

Mom and Jack
start coaching us on how
to play dead.

I thought Will
would be more wiggly
than a gummy worm.

But it turns out
he's even better at lying still
than I am.

And practically a genius
at keeping his eyelids
from fluttering.

When I tell him
what a great actor he is,
he puffs out his skinny little chest

and says, "Being a great actor
ith of paramount importanthe when you're
pulling off a thcam of thith magnitude."

At Seven Thirty p.m.

When we've perfected playing dead,
we begin rehearsing the "scene"—

working out how
we'll wait till Connor arrives,

wait till he sees
the scene of the accident,

with "Greta" weeping
over our bloody bodies,

and Jack (disguised as the drunk driver),
staggering around moaning,

"I've killed them . . .
Oh my God . . . I've killed them!"

And then,
after Mom tells Connor

that I was sending a text (to *him*!)
when it happened,

after she's sobbed
that if I hadn't been so distracted

I might have been able to grab Will
and pull us both to safety,

after we've made Connor suffer
even worse than he made *me* suffer,

I'll squeeze Will's hand,
and that'll be the signal

for us to leap up
and yell in unison,

"Gotcha!"

At Eight p.m.

The extras and the cars show up,
and we get them all into position
out in front of the hotel.

Then Lillian, Oscar, and Mitzi arrive
to transform Mom and Jack,
and slather Will and me with movie blood.

And at nine o'clock,
when everything's ready,
I go off by myself to send the last text.

My thumbs tremble
as I type the words:
The coast is clear.

I thought The Conman
would answer right away.
But he makes me wait for his reply.

And when he *does* text me back,
he says: **Dunno if I can make it.
Might be too busy.**

My Heart Hurls Itself Against My Ribs

Is the fish
I've been reeling in all week
about to get away?

I think fast and text him again:
I bought some stuff from Victoria's Secret.
Don't u want me to model it for u?

I stare at the phone
in the palm of my clammy hand,
willing it to buzz,

but it just lies there—
playing dead even better
than Will.

A Minute Passes

Then two.
Then five.

I tell myself
The Conman's just messing with me.

But I feel like an elephant's
standing on my chest . . .

Could
all this planning,

all these preparations,
all this effort

really have been
for *nothing*?

I Wait Five More Endless Minutes

And the whole while,
I'm racking my brain

to think of something that a snake
like Connor would find irresistible.

And then—
it dawns on me:

**If u come over right now,
I'll give u something really special . . .**

And, finally, he texts me back:
What will u give me?

I keep *him* waiting this time,
letting his curiosity build.

Then I type:
My virginity.

He texts me back right away this time:
You're a virgin?

And I reply:
Yeah. But I won't be after tonight.

And I Guess That Clinches It

Because here's what
his next text says:
I'll be there in ten.

When I see his words
pop onto my screen,
my mouth goes drier than straw.

I text him right back:
**Awesome! Got to walk Will
up to my mom's room,**

**then I'll come back out here
to wait for u
in front of the hote—**

And I make sure
to click send
before I finish the text,

so that
The Conman
will believe "Greta"

when she tells him
that I was in the middle of texting him
when we got run over.

I Hurry Back

To the "scene of the accident,"
and tell everyone
that he's on his way.

Will looks as if I've just announced
that Santa Claus is dropping by
with a sleigh full of early Christmas gifts.

He claps
his hands together sharply,
and says, "Platheth everyone!"

Then he grabs my hand,
pulls me over to where Mom's standing
on the sidewalk with Jack next to the SUV,

and tugs me down,
till the two of us are lying
face-to-bloody-face.

"Thith ith gonna be even more fun
than thcamming waitretheth," he says.
"Yeah," I say. "I guess so . . ."

Though for some strange reason,
my stomach feels like
I'm on a roller coaster,

just before a thousand-foot drop.

Then

We hear
the far-off rumble
of Connor's motorcycle,
thundering up the long winding driveway.

We glance up
and see his headlight
glowing in the distance,
like the beam of a tiny flashlight.

Will can't contain himself.
"Here he comth!" he shouts.
Mom looks down at me, and growls,
"No *way* . . . Connor rides a *motorcycle*?"

Oh, shit . . . *shit* . . .
"Jesus Christ," Mom snaps.
"Have you been riding around
on the back of a *death trap* all summer?"

"Don't be silly . . . ," I say,
scouring my mind for a lie that will
save me from being grounded for life.
And then—Will pipes up.

"Yeah, Mom," he says.
"Don't be thilly. That motorthycle
belongth to hith brother. Connor had to
borrow it becauthe hith car'th broken."

Mom shakes her head in amusement.
"Ohhh . . . ," she says, "No *wonder*.
Your sister had me worried
there for a minute."

Whoa . . .
I never realized, until just now,
what a truly skilled liar
my baby brother has become . . .

A Second Later

Connor's motorcycle vrooms around
the last bend in the driveway.

Will's whole body tenses
with excitement.

He grabs my hand
and whispers, "Thith ith it!"

Then he squeezes his eyes closed,
letting his hand go limp in mine.

And
in two seconds flat,

he looks so lifeless,
so utterly dead

that a little shudder
races up my spine.

Then his eyes pop open again,
and he smiles at me,

the sweetest,
most adoring smile in the world,

and whispers, "When I grow up
I'm gonna be jutht like you.

I'm gonna pull off mega cool thcamth
like thith all the time.

I'm gonna be
famouth for lying!"

Then He Goes Back to Playing Dead

His words
echoing in my head . . .

I glance over and see Jack
snapping into action,

staggering around and groaning,
"Oh my God . . . I've killed them!"

I see "Greta"
wrapping her arms around herself,

letting loose a flood of real tears
(how does she *do* that?) . . .

Then I shift my gaze
back to Connor,

tracking his progress
as he parks his bike in the lot,

climbs down off of it,
and begins closing

the fifty-foot gap
between us,

slowing his pace as he notices
the SUV up on the sidewalk,

and all the flashing lights,
and the horrified onlookers,

hanging back a little
as if he's sort of spooked—

afraid of what he might discover
when he gets close enough to see.

And Then

I look back
at my brother's face.

His eyes are still closed,
but his cheeks are flushed,

and there's this
proud little smirk on his lips.

A smirk that reminds me
of something . . .

reminds me
of the look on . . .

on
Connor's face—

when he told me
he was famous

for lying!

And That's When

Something inside of me
breaks.

It just snaps in two,
like a wishbone.

And before I even
know what I'm doing,

I'm scrambling to my feet, saying,
"Wait . . . wait a minute, everyone!

I don't want to do this!"

Will Sits Up Abruptly

He doesn't say anything.
But he looks as if I've just told him
there's no Tooth Fairy.

I kiss the top of his head,
then turn and march toward Connor,
who's only ten feet away now.

When he sees me,
his irritatingly handsome face
goes pale as chalk.

"Oh my God!" he gasps. "Are you okay?"
"Never been better," I say.
"But you're covered with blood . . . ," he says.

"Oh, you mean *this* stuff?" I say,
rubbing my hands over the sticky red goo
that's drenching the front of my tee.

"This isn't real. It's movie blood.
It was all just part of the scam."
"What scam?" he says, blinking in confusion.

"The scam
where I trick you into believing
that Will and I are dead—

so that you can see
how it feels to be lied to
about something like that."

And Connor's jaw drops open so wide
that it practically scrapes
the sidewalk.

Then He Glances Over
at the "Accident"

And when he looks back at me,
his eyes have narrowed
into two glinting slits.

"Do you mean to tell me," he says,
"that all of this is *fake*?"
"Just as fake as your cancer was," I say.

His hands
ball into fists at his sides.
"Lying's what I do," I say. "Just like you.

But a couple of minutes ago,
when I looked into Will's face,
I knew I had to stop.

So I'm gonna start right now—
by telling you the truth about my age.
I'm not eighteen. I'm fifteen."

"*Fifteen* . . . ?" he gasps.
He takes a quick step back, like he's just
found out I have a contagious disease.

"Jesus Christ . . . ," he says.
"If I'd done it with you,
 it would've been statutory rape!"

"I hadn't thought of that," I say,
nailing him with an icy glare.
"But now I almost wish we *had* slept together—

because then
I could've had you
arrested."

Connor's Eyes Flash

He opens and closes his fists,
like he's just aching to wring my neck.
"You're a real piece of work . . . ," he says.

"It takes one to know one," I say.
"But I don't want to be anything like you.
That's why I called off the scam.

Because if I'd gone through with it,
then I'd be stooping to your level.
And I want to show my brother

there's another way to be."

Suddenly—Will's Standing Beside Me

He slips his hand into mine,
looks up at me solemnly, and says,
"I don't want to thtoop to hith level either."

I pull him in
for a quick fierce hug.
Then he turns to Connor and says,

"But I sure wish
I could've theen the look on your fathe
when you thaw our corptheth."

Connor clenches his teeth.
"I've had it up to *here*," he sneers,
"with that cutesy little lisp of yours."

"And we've had it up to here
with *you*!" I say.
"We thertainly have!" Will says.

Then, before Connor can say another word,
the two of us turn our backs on him
and walk away.

As We Head Toward the SUV

Will slips his hand
into mine again.

Then he looks up at me,
as innocent as anything,

and asks,
"What'th thtatutory rape?"

"I'll tell you later," I say.
"When you're twelve."

"Oh, forget it," he says.
"I'll jutht athk Mom."

After

After we've thanked
the prop guys and the extras
and sent them all home,

and after
Mom and Jack have told us
how proud they are of us,

and after
Will and I have scrubbed off
every last bit of blood,

I lock myself in the bathroom,
and remove my purple contacts.
Then—I flush them down the toilet.

I peer at myself in the mirror,
stare into my hazel eyes,
and make myself a promise:

"No. More. Lies."

But That's Much Easier *Said* Than Done

At first it seems as if
whenever I open my mouth
another whopper pops out,

like those moles do,
when you're playing
that Whac-A-Mole game.

Half the time,
I don't even realize I've *told* another lie,
until Will points it out.

He gets right up in my face
and says, "There you go again—
telling another thtory . . ."

And I do the same for Will,
whenever I catch *him*
telling a lie.

He's even made
progress charts
for us.

And we stick shiny gold stars onto them
(*and* treat ourselves to a couple of Oreos)
whenever we show "thigns of improvement."

Then Finally

After about a week,
both of us manage to go a whole hour
without telling a single lie.

And a few days after that,
we succeed in spending
a completely fib-free afternoon.

And today,
we somehow made it through
the whole day without any lapses.

But just now, when Mom asked us
who ate all the Oreos from the minibar,
Will and I both said, "Not me!"

Then we turned
to look at each other
and burst into hysterics.

A Few Days Later

At the end
of the very last day of filming,
Jack shows up and says he wants
to take us all out to dinner at Shangri-la.

But then he does something weird—
he tells Mom that he needs
five minutes alone
with Will and me first.

She gives him a funny look.
Then shrugs and says, "Sure . . .
Why not? You guys head down
and I'll catch up in a few."

Shit . . .
Mom's probably dumped Jack already,
and he just wants a chance
to say good-bye to us.

When we get downstairs
to the restaurant and settle into
one of the insanely pink booths,
Jack suddenly gets all misty-eyed.

Oh no . . .
Here it comes . . .
Then, he takes a deep breath,
and I swear to God this is true,

he says, "I'd like to ask
your mother to marry me.
But not unless you kids
think it's a good idea."

"Wow!" Will says,
"Does that mean you want to be our dad?"
"It would be my honor," Jack says.
And when I hear these words,

my heart dances up into my throat.

I Can't Speak

So I give Jack
two thumbs up.
And Will does too.

Jack grins at us,
heaves a massive sigh of relief,
then pulls us into his arms.

I nestle
into the comforting
dad-ness of him.

But that's when my heart crumbles.
Because I realize that I've gotten
my hopes up way too high.

I mean, this is *Mom*
he's planning on proposing to.
She's not exactly the marrying kind.

What if she turns him down?
Aw, who am I kidding?
She's *gonna* turn him down . . .

And when she does,
Will's gonna be
totally devastated.

And,
okay,
I admit it—

I will be too.

A Second Later, Mom Walks Into the Restaurant

Jack leaps up from the booth
so that she can slide in next to us.

I glance
at my brother's face.

He looks deliriously happy,
the poor little guy . . .

Then,
Jack pulls a tiny box out of his pocket,

gets down on one knee,
and asks Mom to marry him.

Her hand
flies up to her throat,

and she makes
this strange little choking sound.

I grab hold of Will's hand under the table
and squeeze tight.

But then Mom throws her arms
around Jack's neck

and says,
"Yes! Yes yes yes yes *yes!*"

And everyone in the restaurant
bursts into applause,

just like in one of those über corny scenes
from one of Mom's movies.

After Jack Slips the Ring
Onto Her Finger

And after they stop
kissing each other,

and the applause
finally winds down,

the waitress comes over
and takes our order.

But as she heads away from our table,
Will steals a glance at me,

then dashes after her,
tugs on her sleeve,

and whispers something
in her ear . . .

But Don't Worry

Will and I aren't up
to our old tricks again.

It really *is*
my birthday.

I'm sixteen years old
today.

And this is one birthday
I'll never forget.

When We're Through With Dinner

The waitress doesn't bring me
a free dessert.

She brings me a whole entire cake.
Mom ordered it special.

She smiles at me and says,
"Did you think I'd forgotten?"

After I blow out the candles,
it's time for presents.

Jack gives me a pair of silver earrings
shaped like the Eiffel Tower.

Then Mom hands me
a thin gold box.

And when I open it,
I find a round-trip ticket to Paris!

Mom says the four of us are leaving
tomorrow for a two-week vacation.

I squeal with delight
and hug them both.

Then Will says,
"And here'th *my* prethent."

I tear off the paper
and find a blank book to write in.

He says he's going to miss
all my stories,

but at least now
if I think of a mega cool one,

I'll have a place
to write it down if I want.

Which is when
I have

my epiphany.

Full Disclosure

To be perfectly honest,
I don't think I'll *ever* be able
to be perfectly honest.

But
the truth is,
I don't really want to.

I mean, reinventing reality
and spinning it off
in a whole new direction

will probably always be
the most fun I can have
with my clothes on.

So I've figured out a way
to channel all those "creative" urges
of mine:

I've
decided
to become

an author.

In Fact

Maybe
you've just read

my
first book . . .